LUKE SUTTON:
BOUNTY HUNTER

By Leo P. Kelley

LUKE SUTTON:
BOUNTY HUNTER

LEO P. KELLEY

DOUBLEDAY & COMPANY, INC.
GARDEN CITY, NEW YORK
1985

All of the characters in this book
are fictitious, and any resemblance
to actual persons, living or dead,
except for historical personages,
is purely coincidental.

Library of Congress Cataloging in Publication Data

Kelley, Leo P.
Luke Sutton, bounty hunter.

I. Title.
PS3561.E388L827 1985   813'.54
ISBN: 0-385-19900-7
Library of Congress Catalog Card Number 85-7054
Copyright © 1985 by Leo P. Kelley
All Rights Reserved
Printed in the United States of America

First Edition

WITHDRAWN

FROM COLLECTION

ONE

The hot water, from which tendrils of steam snaked upward, soothed Luke Sutton's body as he sat in the tin bathtub, his eyes closed, his muscles relaxed, and his mind almost at ease.

He sighed, a soft sound of contentment, and leaned back against the tub for a long dreamy moment. Then, opening his eyes and sitting upright, he began to wash his body vigorously, his nostrils tantalized by the pervasive scent of lemon verbena that came from the bar of soap in his hand. He picked up a stiff-bristled brush that lay on the table beside the tub and began to scrub his body to rid it of every last vestige of trail dust and desert sand, both of which had plagued him during the past several weeks.

Ah, he thought, it's good to be— Home? But this, he thought as he looked around his room in Virginia City's International Hotel—this here's not home. It's a far cry from it. All it is is where I light when what I've got to do's done. It's where I go to ground when there's nothing goading me. But home?

He shook his head, and as he stood up in the tub, suds streamed down his lean and rawboned body. Nope, he thought. This here rented room of mine's not a home, not by a long shot it's not. What it is is, it's just a burrow to come back to, a den I can hole up in from time to time when life lets me be.

He bent over, scooped up water in both cupped hands and used it to rinse the frothy suds from his body. As he did so, his eyes fell on the dodger that he had earlier in the day placed on the table beside the tub. The dodger was the reason why, despite the fact that the hot bath he had just taken had soothed and almost lulled him into slumber, his mind was not completely at ease.

The dodger, with its words and picture of a wanted man printed on it and its offer of a thousand-dollar bounty for the return of the fugitive either dead or alive, was a silent challenge hurled at him, a lure dangled before him, a snare placed in his path.

He picked up a thick towel that lay draped over the back of an overstuffed armchair and began to dry himself.

Sutton was a tall man who seemed even taller when unencumbered, as he was at the moment, by any clothes. His body, as lean as it was lithe, was marred here and there by scars, some of them ragged red lines, others livid welts of dead flesh, each of them mutely telling its own painful story of hot lead ripping through skin and bone, or of the sharp bite of a sadistically wielded bullwhip, or of the fiery torture devised by a Comanche warrior in a long-ago and now nearly forgotten time.

His shoulders were broad and his chest was thick. Both were masses of muscle and sinew. His hips were narrow, almost bony, beneath the flat expanse of his belly. His legs, sturdy and strong, seemed to anchor him to the earth, and his arms were slender but sturdy blendings of muscle and bone which ended in the large and strong-fingered hands that he had more than once been forced to use as highly effective defensive weapons.

His face was as lean and rawboned as his body, almost gaunt. None of his features, noted individually, were in any way remarkable. His forehead was broad, and his straight black hair, which hid his ears and the nape of his neck, tended to tumble down over it. His deep-set eyes were the color of woodsmoke. His nose was straight, his lips a thin lean line, his jaw square, and his cheeks were slightly sunken valleys beneath the prominent ridges of his cheekbones. But his individual features, each unremarkable by itself, combined in a stark and striking way to give him a face which, once seen, was not easily forgotten. His was the alert-eyed face of the dedicated hunter, the always somber, sometimes grim, face of a man who has seen more than his share of the ugly and the awful events that the world can unleash upon a man with no warning. A haunted and haunting face was Sutton's.

He stepped out of the tub and, hopping first on one foot and then the other, finished drying himself. Then, dropping his towel on the chair, he yawned and stretched, his fingers reaching for the ceiling as he stood on the tips of his toes, the many muscles in his body tensing, rippling, and finally relaxing.

As he began to dress, the clothes he put on felt strange to him, almost uncomfortable in their newness. He had bought them earlier that day after he had returned to Virginia City from Arizona Territory. When he had finished dressing, Sutton studied himself in the mirror, his eyes roving from his shiny black shoes, up his black-and-white-checked trousers, over his white shirt beneath his sack coat, to his white paper collar and black string tie, and finally to the black derby hat that he had perched at a decidedly rakish angle on his head.

Now don't I look the citified dude though, he thought, grinning into the mirror. It's for sure nobody'd ever spot me for a fiddle-footed Texas stump-jumper who's far from home and hearth. His grin widened.

Then, after touching the brim of his derby in a roguish salute to his reflection, he picked up the dodger, pocketed it, and left the room. He boarded the hydraulic elevator and emerged from it into the hotel's ornate lobby that was a somewhat garish blend of red velvet, polished brass, and mohair.

He made his way to the desk, where he told the desk clerk, "You can send somebody up to get the bathtub out of my room now."

"Yes, sir. Right away, sir." The desk clerk, an elderly man, briskly rang the bell to summon a smartly uniformed youngster who was standing not far away.

"Have him pick up the clothes I left in a pile on the floor too," Sutton added. "They're badly in need of laundering."

As the desk clerk gave orders to the bellboy, Sutton made his way across the lobby, down the hall, and into the hotel's sumptuous bar. He found an empty table at the far end of the room, and when a white-aproned waiter appeared before him, he ordered whiskey.

When the waiter had brought his drink, Sutton sipped it while surveying the room in search of the man he had earlier arranged to meet.

But William Wright, editor of Virginia City's *Territorial Enterprise* and writer for that newspaper under the pen name of Dan DeQuille, did not arrive in the bar until nearly an hour after Sutton had. He stood in the open doorway, peering into the smoky room, and then, when he spotted Sutton at the far end of the room, he waved and hurried toward him. Seating himself across from Sutton, he drew a white linen handkerchief from his pocket and wiped his sweaty forehead. "Luke, I'm sorry I'm late, but I'm afraid I couldn't help it. We had a last-minute story that had to be substituted on the front page and a goodly part of tomorrow's run had already been printed when the change was made."

"You're here now, Bill, and that's what matters. What'll you have?"

Wright beckoned, and when a waiter arrived at the table, he ordered, "Cognac." Then, turning to Sutton, he said, "What now, Luke?"

Sutton raised an eyebrow.

"Don't look at me in that arch way of yours, Luke. I know very well you won't be staying in town very long. You'll be off again somewhere for some reason and no words of wisdom from me or anyone else will stay your going. Am I right?"

In answer to Wright's question, Sutton pulled the dodger from his pocket, unfolded it, and spread it out on top of the green-baize-covered table. "You're to blame this time, Bill. It was you yourself who went and pointed out this dodger to me only this afternoon right after I got back to town. So if I decide to head out after this mister, well, like I said, this time it's your fault, so don't you start braying to me about how I go about making my way in the world."

Wright clucked his tongue and declared, "You're no sooner back after having had a run-in with Geronimo and his reservation-jumping renegade Apaches down in Arizona Territory than here you are biting at the bit and wanting to set out on the trail of that outlaw."

"It says there," Sutton remarked, tapping the dodger with the tip of his right index finger, "that Theodore Kimball's wanted for murdering somebody by the name of Dade McGrath a little over two weeks ago. What might you happen to know about that matter, Bill, that just might help me catch Kimball and put a stop to his murdering ways?"

"Ted Kimball," Wright said, sadly shaking his head, "was a highly respected and very successful lawyer who practiced here in Virginia City ever since he graduated from Harvard Law School back in '71. But he had a hot temper the same as his father before him did, God rest Ted Senior's soul."

Sutton waited, sipping his whiskey, his eyes on Wright.

"Ted Kimball, during the time he lived and practiced law here in town, had struck up an acquaintance with a woman named Fern Thorndyke," Wright continued and then fell silent until the waiter who had brought the cognac he had ordered departed. "The long and the short of it is Ted fell head over heels in love with the Thorndyke woman. She was—is—a beauty.

"Dade McGrath, who owned several businesses here in town and a controlling interest in the Nugget Mine, took an interest in Miss Thorndyke, and to make a long story short if not sweet, Kimball, on a visit to town from his new base of operations in San Francisco, found McGrath with Miss Thorndyke. Apparently, McGrath was forcing his attentions upon the lady. Ted, in his characteristically hot-blooded fashion, struck McGrath on the head with a poker, killing the man instantly. After the murder Ted disappeared, and he hasn't been seen since. At least not by anyone who's willing to say he saw the fugitive."

"A crime of passion," Sutton mused, emptying his glass.

"I told you Ted Kimball had a temper."

"Most murderers do, I've noticed. It's what goads them into killing. Now about this Kimball—he have relatives here or anywhere that anybody knows about?"

The woman said she did not and closed the door.

Sutton made his way back down the incline of A Street and, again following Wright's directions, located the office of Marcus Proctor in the heart of Virginia City's business district. He climbed the outside stairs and entered the second-floor office, where he found himself confronting a bespectacled clerk whose narrow skull seemed perched atop his blindingly white paper collar.

"May I be of service, sir?" the man inquired in a reedy voice.

"You may," Sutton responded. "I'd like to have a talk with your boss."

"Have you an appointment?"

"Nope."

"Mr. Proctor is engaged at the moment. Shall I make an appointment for you to call back at some other mutually convenient time?"

Ignoring the clerk's question, Sutton strode around the side of the man's desk.

"I say, sir!" the clerk exclaimed, starting to rise from his swivel chair. "You can't—"

"I can," Sutton said as he reached out, clapped a hand on the clerk's right shoulder, and forcibly reseated the spluttering man. With his free hand he opened the door directly behind the clerk's desk.

Once inside the larger office, he slammed the door and said, "My name's Luke Sutton. You, I take it, are Marcus Proctor."

The portly man seated behind the desk peered through the folds of his narrowed eyes at Sutton, both of his fat hands filled with papers. Then, his jowls quivering as he spoke, he asked, "What do you mean by barging in here unannounced in such a discourteous and unprofessional manner?"

"He had no brothers or sisters. His mother had predeceased her husband by five years and Ted Senior died in January last year of galloping pneumonia. There may be aunts and uncles—some cousins somewhere—but if there are, no one around here can recall ever hearing Ted Senior or his son mention them."

"But there's Kimball's lady friend."

"Miss Fern Thorndyke, yes."

"I think I'll have myself a talk with her. She might be able to tell me something helpful about how to run down Kimball, wherever he might be at the moment. Bill, is there anybody else who might know something about Kimball's whereabouts and be willing to pass along what they know to me?"

Wright thoughtfully stroked his black beard. "There's Marcus Proctor."

"Who's Marcus Proctor?"

"Proctor's a stockbroker—mining stock mostly—here in Virginia City. He handled the Kimball family's investments. But the sheriff talked to Proctor after the killing, and Proctor claims to know nothing of the present whereabouts of Kimball."

"I reckon I'd best pay a call on Mr. Proctor too once I'm through talking to Miss Thorndyke."

"Then you've made up your mind, Luke? You're going out after Ted Kimball?"

"A thousand dollars is a lot of money, Bill. For a man like me with no visible means of support, it would come in mighty handy and just might make me seem like maybe I'm first cousin to respectable despite my shiftless ways." Sutton grinned.

Wright didn't. "Kimball's killed once and will hang for that dark deed if he's caught by you or anyone else. I've little doubt he'll do his damnedest to kill any bounty hunter he finds traveling his back trail. You know that, don't you, Luke?"

"I do, Bill. But like I said, a thouand dollars is a hefty, if not exactly princely, sum of bounty money, and I could sure use it, so I reckon I'll set out to see if I can't collect it."

"Kimball might kill you."

Sutton nodded. "He might."

"Why not leave Kimball to others?" Wright prodded, downing his drink. "Stay here in town. Get a job somewhere. There are lots of people who would hire you. People who know your many good qualities. Isn't it time you settled down, Luke, and let yourself just sit back and enjoy the good things in life?"

"Bill, it seems to me that a man—most men maybe—are pretty much fashioned on the last of the life they've lived. It—whatever kind of life it was they've lived—it's bent and shaped them till they haven't got much of a choice anymore in the trails they travel or the way they travel them. Take me, for instance. I was pretty much settled down years ago in Texas. Then—well, you know what happened to change things for me."

"But that's all behind you now, Luke. You caught up with the men who murdered your brother. You wanted vengeance and—"

"I got it." Something flared briefly in Sutton's eyes, something dark and ugly, and then it was gone as quickly as it had come. "But in the getting, Bill, something happened to me. Now it seems I've always got to be on the move. Got to see what's over the mountain and up the crick. Something died in me the day my brother was murdered. But something was born at the selfsame time. Something—I'm hard put to find a name for it. It's—call it a kind of hunger. For new trails, new towns, strange

faces, and unexpected things happening all the time. I like the way I've been living these past three, four years. It's not a life you could exactly call respectable, but it's one that's got some spice to it."

"It's a risky life. In point of fact, a downright dangerous one."

"Bill, what else am I to do given the truth I've just told you about how there's something in my blood that drives me on and just won't let me light anywhere for long?"

"You've got—"

"A room in this here hotel and that's all. Four walls with a whole lot of lonely space in between them."

Wright sighed and beckoned to the waiter. "I guess all that's left for me to do is to offer a toast to the success of your impending manhunt."

Later, when both men had fresh drinks in their hands, Wright raised his glass and said, "Luck, Luke."

"A man like me can always use some of that scarce commodity, Bill."

Both men drank then, their voices silent, their faces solemn.

After breakfasting on steak and eggs the following morning in the hotel's ornate dining room, Sutton set out to pay a visit to Fern Thorndyke. By following the directions Wright had given him the night before, he readily located the woman's boarding house halfway up the slope of Mount Davidson on A Street.

The door was opened in response to his knock by an elderly woman with white hair and cheeks as plump and rosy as apples.

"Is Miss Fern Thorndyke to home?" Sutton inquired, and was told that Miss Thorndyke had "stepped out."

"Do you maybe know when the lady'll be back?"

Sutton seated himself in the chair in front of Proctor's desk. "I apologize for busting in on you like I've just done, but I'm a busy man, Mr. Proctor. Now I know you're as busy—most likely even busier'n me, so let's us get right down to cases. I'd be obliged to you if you'd tell me where I might find Ted Kimball."

Proctor dropped the papers he had been holding and stared at Sutton. Then, leaning back in his chair, he interlaced his pudgy fingers and placed both of his interlocked hands on his ample paunch. "What is the nature of your business with Mr. Kimball, may I be so bold as to ask?"

"He's worth a thousand dollars to me."

"Ah, so you're a bounty hunter."

"At the moment, yep, I am, I reckon."

"I know nothing of the whereabouts of Mr. Kimball. If I did know where he was, I certainly would not tell you, Mr.— What did you say your name was?"

"Sutton. Luke Sutton. Now why would a law-abiding businessman such as yourself, Mr. Proctor, not want to cooperate with a man like me who's out to collar Kimball and see that he pays the price he owes the law for what he went and did to the late lamented Mr. Dade Mc-Grath?"

"I feel that I must tell you that I have nothing but contempt for bounty hunters like you, Mr. Sutton. I find them despicable as individuals and I find their profession a blatant disgrace to a supposedly civilized society. Bounty hunters are, Mr. Sutton, by and large nothing more than murderers, in my considered opinion, and as such they are of no greater moral stature than the outlaws whom they have chosen to stalk for purely monetary gain."

"Now that you've gone and spoken your piece, Proctor, let me speak mine. You can have yourself all the contempt for me that you want to, but I got to tell you that what you think means less to me than a pitcher of warm spit. I came here to ask you nice and polite for any help you might give me, and all I've got so far for my trouble is a string of insults as long as my arm.

"I figure now's about time you set aside your insulting ways and started passing out information about Kimball. You don't and I'm just liable to rear up real high on my hind legs and start tearing apart this fancy office of yours."

"You wouldn't dare do such a barbaric thing!"

"Oh, I'd dare all right." Sutton stood up swiftly, deliberately sending the chair he had been sitting in crashing to the floor behind him. He picked up a glass paperweight from Proctor's desk. "I'll put this thing clear through that window behind you, Proctor, if you don't start talking fast to me about Ted Kimball."

Proctor's gaze shifted from Sutton's stern expression to the paperweight in his hand and then back to Sutton's face. "The Kimball family has done business with my firm for many years."

When Proctor hesitated, Sutton's hand that held the glass paperweight rose slightly.

"Through me Ted has invested," Proctor said hurriedly, "in the stock of several of the Comstock Lode's silver mines."

Sutton put the paperweight down on the desk. He picked up his overturned chair and sat down. Listening to Proctor during the next several minutes, he learned that Theodore Kimball had opened a legal office in San Francisco nearly a year earlier, that he had lost a great deal of money on some of his investments when two of the mines in which he owned shares had gone out of

business, that what Proctor called "this temporary decline in the Lode's fortunes" would surely end soon, and
that Proctor did not know where Kimball could be found
but he would gladly give Sutton the address of Kimball's
office in San Francisco if Sutton so desired.

"I'd be obliged to you," Sutton declared and accepted
the scrap of paper on which Proctor had jotted the address. After glancing at it and then pocketing it, he asked,
"What made Kimball pull up stakes here and head west
to San Francisco?"

Proctor smiled. "Young love, Mr. Sutton, is a truly
wondrous thing."

"What's that supposed to mean?"

"Ted had fallen in love with a Miss Fern Thorndyke,
and they had decided, he told me, to move to San Francisco once Ted's fledgling law practice was solidly estab-
lished there and they had been married. Apparently,
they both considered San Francisco a far more sophisti-
cated metropolis than our own Virginia City, despite the
presence here of Piper's Opera House and—"

Sutton rose and headed for the door.

"Before you go, Mr. Sutton."

Sutton turned to face Proctor, who had risen to his
feet.

"Assuming you are successful in locating and apprehending Ted Kimball, Mr. Sutton, do you—there is just
no delicate way to put this—do you intend to kill him?"

A muscle in Sutton's jaw jumped. "I'll answer you this
way, Proctor. I intend to get Kimball—dead or alive."

TWO

Sutton next paid a call on Sheriff Morley Hoskins, who, as Sutton entered the man's office, waved a hand in greeting from where he sat behind his battered wooden desk and declared, "It's good to see you again, Luke. What brings you here?"

"Ted Kimball, Morley. He's what brings me here."

Hoskins pulled a pouch of Bull Durham and a packet of brown papers from his pocket and began to build a cigarette before inquiring, "What have you got to do with Kimball, Luke, or do I already know the answer to that question?"

"I reckon you do know it, Morley. Yesterday, Bill Wright pointed out a dodger to me that had Kimball's picture on it along with the fact that he's worth a thousand dollars in bounty money. I thought I'd try to run the man to ground and then turn him over to you. But to do that I need to know as much about him as I can learn. So I thought I'd come by here and see what you could maybe tell me about him and the crime he committed."

"It's kind of funny how things work out in this old world of ours," Hoskins mused, and lit his cigarette.

"I'm not sure I follow you, Morley."

"I was thinking that you yourself were a wanted man not so long ago, and now here you are all set to go out after another wanted man. Kind of ironic, you might say."

"Ironic it well may be, Morley, but as far as I'm concerned, this is just a business matter I've decided to see to. I want to earn that thousand dollars the law's offering for Kimball."

"It's not the law that's offering the reward to any man who can catch up with Kimball," Hoskins declared, and then took a deep drag on his cigarette. After blowing a smoke ring into the air, he continued, "It's a bunch of civic-minded citizens here in town, led by Dade McGrath's brother Lorne, who've put up the bounty money. McGrath was a businessman highly thought of here in Virginia City, and his murder, well, it's touched off the ire of some pretty prominent citizens, not to mention that of his blood kin, Lorne McGrath. It's them, led by Lorne, who've pooled their resources and come up with the bounty money. They're willing to pay to see to it that McGrath's murderer hangs."

"It don't much matter to me where the money comes from, Morley. What matters to me is that I get to collect it. And that's where you come into the picture. Like I said before, I'd be obliged if you'd tell me what you know about Kimball and about what happened. All I know about the matter so far is that Kimball killed McGrath on account of McGrath was paying heed to a lady friend of Kimball's."

"That's about the long and the short of it, Luke. Kimball and Fern Thorndyke, they were real close, like a peach and its pit. In fact, they were talking about getting hitched, that pair was. But then Kimball happened upon McGrath and the Thorndyke woman together, and I guess he didn't like what he saw, and there was a fight and Kimball killed McGrath."

"With a poker."

"You've been checking things out, have you? Yep, it was a poker Kimball used to brain McGrath with."

"Where exactly did the crime take place, Morley?"

"In McGrath's office just down the street."

"What was Miss Thorndyke doing in McGrath's office? Did she tell you?"

"She did. It seems McGrath had loaned her some money to set up a ladies' millinery business. She'd come to pay back the balance of what she owed him. Ted Kimball had given her the money to pay off McGrath because he didn't cotton to the idea of the woman he loved being bound in any make, shape, or form to another man. Especially one like McGrath."

" 'Especially one like McGrath,' Morley? Now what might you mean by that remark?"

"Dade McGrath—it's common knowledge, so I'm not telling tales out of school—was a notorious womanizer, and Fern Thorndyke, well, she's a pretty package, and the combination was about as potentially explosive as dynamite. I guess Kimball could see that, and he wanted his woman to be free of any kind of connection to McGrath."

Sutton recalled Bill Wright's remark about McGrath having taken an interest in Fern Thorndyke. "Did Kimball go to McGrath's office with Miss Thorndyke?"

Hoskins shook his head. "He waited outside for her, but when she seemed to be taking longer than he thought was proper for her to complete her business with McGrath, he went barging into the office after her and—well, I already told you what happened next."

"I take it you got the story of what happened from Miss Thorndyke?"

"Not at first, I didn't. At first, she gave me a cock-and-bull story about a burglar who'd burst into McGrath's office to rob him. She claimed the two men—McGrath and the robber—scuffled and the robber wound up clouting McGrath with the poker and killing him. That woman tried her damnedest to protect Ted Kimball, I will say that much for her."

"I kind of get the feeling you're not too keen on Fern Thorndyke, Morley."

Hoskins harrumphed. "She's a smooth one, she is, and a thoroughly accomplished liar, I'll tell you that. But what I think of her doesn't matter one way or the other.

"Anyway, I found somebody who'd seen Kimball go into McGrath's office. That man—he sells fresh produce from a wagon and was in the neighborhood near McGrath's office—he told me he heard voices—the voices of two men—and the next thing he sees Kimball run out of McGrath's office 'like all the devils in hell were after him' was the way he put it to me.

"Well, after I heard that story, I took myself back to Fern Thorndyke and she called the produce man a liar. She swore Kimball had never been in McGrath's office. I badgered her as best I could, but she held tight to her story. It wasn't till I went and questioned Marcus Proctor—for the third time—about Ted Kimball and his relationship with Fern Thorndyke and her relationship with McGrath in the hopes of turning up something—anything, since I was about backed up against the wall at that point and getting nowhere fast—that Proctor broke down and admitted to me that Kimball had come to him right after the murder. Kimball, Proctor finally admitted to me, was all upset and said he needed cash money and he needed it in a hurry. Proctor said he gave him money out of Kimball's own brokerage account. But the most important thing that Proctor told me the third time I talked to him was that Kimball confessed to him that he'd just up and murdered Dade McGrath because he'd caught the man making advances to Fern Thorndyke.

"Well, I went and had another talk with the Thorndyke woman. I confronted her with what Proctor had just told me, and she finally admitted that what Kimball had told Proctor about what had happened in McGrath's office was the truth. She said Kimball had told her after he'd killed McGrath that he was going to Proctor for the money he needed to make his getaway. I gather he was short of cash after giving Fern the money to pay off McGrath. She, in turn, told him that she'd do her best to cover up for him, and she did a pretty good job of it at first with the lies about that nonexistent burglar she told me. So there it all was at last, Luke, laid out for me as plain as apple pie."

Sutton nodded thoughtfully.

"It's really a damned shame about Kimball," Hoskins mused. "He was a real nice fellow. Never was in any trouble before—not before he killed McGrath. He had himself a real promising future. He was a good lawyer like his father before him. People trusted him the same way they'd always trusted Ted Senior. Him and Miss Thorndyke were, like I said before, talking about tying the knot. Then Kimball goes and lets his temper get the best of him, and all of a sudden his life and his whole future—well, now neither one's worth a plugged nickel. A damned shame! But a man's got to pay the price for what he does in this life; there's no getting around that fact."

"I'm obliged to you, Morley, for your time and the information you've seen fit to give me."

"Always glad to be of help to a good friend. Now you take care, you hear me, Luke? I guess though I don't need to tell you that Kimball's a desperate man. He's killed once and he'll kill again, I've no doubt, if he has to in order to keep himself from having a face-to-face meeting with the hangman."

"Be seeing you, Morley."

After leaving the sheriff's office, Sutton made his way back up the slope of Mount Davidson, walking briskly along A Street until he came once again to the door of Fern Thorndyke's boardinghouse. He knocked, and the woman who had earlier opened the door did so again.

"Miss Fern Thorndyke," Sutton said. "She here?"

The woman glanced over her shoulder into the dim interior of the house and then, looking back at Sutton and frowning, she said, "She's here. But not for much longer, may the saints be praised. I run a respectable house—always did until now. A widow woman like me has to watch her step. She can't go renting rooms to just any baggage who has the money to pay and then winds up getting herself mixed up in the midst of murder like some I could name if I'd a mind to, but, being a Christian woman, I won't."

"Will you point me the way to Miss Thorndyke's room, ma'am?" Sutton inquired, pushing past the land-lady, who, after muttering, "Well, I never!" and "The nerve of some people!" nevertheless then directed Sutton to a room on the third floor.

When he reached it, he knocked on its door and then, when the door opened, he studied the woman who stood staring at him, a questioning expression on her face.

She was nearly as tall as he was, with a slender but well-proportioned figure which, in combination with her attractive face, would, Sutton was sure, be more than enough to turn the heads of most men the woman passed on the street. There was a subtle allure about her, a pro-vocative quality which, Sutton decided, came from the

faintly seductive way she held herself and the slight tilt
to her head as she continued staring at him.

Her hair, worn in tightly rolled sausage curls, was the
color of ripe corn and it, along with the paleness of her
skin, made her blue eyes almost startling in their intensity. Her lips were full and her nose was pert. She wore a
royal blue chambray dress which had panels of yellow
silk in its skirt and long sleeves that were puffed at the
shoulders. The chambray matched the color of her wide
eyes, and its yellow panels were the same bright color as
her hair.

"Miss Thorndyke?"

"Yes?"

"My name's Luke Sutton, and I've come here to have a
talk with you if you've no objections."

"Objections? As a matter of fact, I do have objections
to talking to strangers. I have found of late and to my
sorrow that strangers can be unkind—sometimes quite
painfully cruel. And you, Mr. Sutton, are a stranger to
me. So if you don't mind—"

Sutton swiftly thrust out a foot which he wedged between the jamb and the door that Fern had tried to close
on him. "Miss Thorndyke, I've come to talk to you on
account of I'm hoping you can help me. And by lending
me a hand with the matter I've got in mind, you can also
help a good friend of yours. A friend name of Ted Kimball."

"Ted? How can I help him, Mr. Sutton? Tell me
quickly. I'll do anything I can to help Ted. What is it you
want me to do?"

"To start out with, you can let me come in and then
maybe the two of us can sit down and have ourselves a
real nice visit."

Once inside the room, Sutton seated himself on a chair

near the door and Fern sat facing him in a chair next to the room's single window.

"How can I help Ted, Mr. Sutton?" she asked eagerly, leaning forward slightly in her chair, her eyes on Sutton's.

"Well, you know there's a price on his head." Sutton saw Fern flinch, but his face remained impassive. "There's liable to be, like as not, some bounty hunters who've gone out after Kimball, since over two weeks have passed since he murdered Dade McGrath."

Fern's body went rigid. As she turned away from Sutton, the sun streaming through the window brightened the left side of her face but left the right side in deep shadow.

"One of those bounty hunters I'm talking about," Sutton continued, "just might wind up killing Kimball."

Fern slowly turned her head until she was facing Sutton again. "I don't think I follow you. Are you offering to protect Ted from any bounty hunters who might be after him?"

"Nope. All I'm doing is saying that a whole lot of bounty hunters would, as a general rule of thumb, just as soon kill their quarry as spit. But not me. I'm not that kind of man."

Fern frowned.

"What I'm getting at here, Miss Thorndyke, is that I'm going out hunting Ted Kimball."

"You mean—you're a bounty hunter?"

"I am now and for the first time where Kimball's concerned. What I was getting at before is that were you to tell me where I might find him, I can promise you that, unlike some other men who might be trailing Kimball, I'll try real hard not to have to kill him. If you could put me onto him, Miss Thorndyke, I'll promise you that I'll do my level best to bring him back alive if he'll let me."

Fern started to rise from her chair, but then she dropped back down upon it and glared at Sutton. "Get out of here!"

Sutton, ignoring her command, reached out and patted the half-filled suitcase lying open on the bed beside him. "Your landlady told me you weren't going to be around here much longer. You're planning to take a trip, are you, Miss Thorndyke?"

"That, sir, is none of your business!"

"It could prove to be a part of my business—if you're off to hook up with Kimball, wherever he might be, since I've already told you I'm bound and determined to collect that thousand dollars bounty money. I know the pair of you were fixing to get married."

Fern turned again and stared blindly out the open window. "I love Ted a great deal, Mr. Sutton. And he loves me as much. We were so happy together. We'd been looking forward to being happy together for the rest of our lives."

Fern hid her face in her hands. Her shoulders shook as she sobbed. When she looked up again, sunlight struck a tear that had oozed from her left eye and set colors—red, green and yellow—to blazing in it. "I tried my best to protect Ted from the law. I even lied for him." She faced Sutton directly, her wet eyes blazing. "And I'd do it again. I'd lie, cheat, deceive. *I would.* I'd do anything to save Ted. It's not his fault, what happened. If anything, it was that disgusting Mr. McGrath's fault. The way he pawed me. The awful things he said to me—dared suggest to me. It's no wonder at all that Ted lost his temper when he burst in upon us and saw—

"In France, Mr. Sutton, such a crime of passion is

often considered excusable and the person who commits it is not punished. But then the Gallic temperament evidently understands the vagaries of love better than we Americans do."

"I don't want to have to kill Kimball, Miss Thorndyke. I thought that if you'd tell me where I might find him— well, I figured maybe I could get the drop on him before he does anything else foolish and then I could let him know that you put me onto him on account of how you had his best interests at heart."

"Were you to apprehend Ted and were you to return him to Virginia City to stand trial, he would not stand a chance. Not with the way Lorne McGrath has stirred up the community until Virginia City—its citizens—have become like a pack of savage hounds baying for poor Ted's blood to appease their thirst for revenge. Mr. Sutton, I will tell you nothing."

"That's a shame, that is, and I'm sorry to hear it," Sutton said, assuming a doleful expression and making his voice mournful. "On account of there's a lot I'd like you to tell me."

Fern said nothing, her lips set in a tightly compressed line.

"Like why you're taking a trip at this particular time and where you're planning on taking it to."

When Fern's eyes darted past Sutton and alarm flared in them, he turned in the direction of her glance and noticed her reticule resting on the top of a bureau that stood against the wall behind him. He rose and went to the dresser where he picked up her reticule and opened it.

"Don't!" Fern cried from behind him, and then she rose and, dashing across the room, tried to tear the reticule from his grasp.

Sutton fended her off with one hand while with the other he dumped the contents of the reticule on top of the dresser. From the jumble made by two iron keys, a tiny bottle of scent, a packet of mints, a lace handkerchief, some coins, and some folding money, he plucked an envelope that was postmarked San Francisco and addressed to Miss Fern Thorndyke.

"How dare you invade a lady's privacy like this," Fern cried, and struck Sutton a blow that glanced off his shoulder. "Give me that letter. Give it to me and get out of my room this instant!" She tried in vain to tear the letter from Sutton's hands.

Turning his back on Fern and oblivious of her small fists pummeling his back and shoulders, he removed the unsigned letter from its envelope, which bore no return address, and hastily read its message, which consisted of only six words: "Come as soon as you can."

He turned to face Fern, and as he did so, she snatched the letter and envelope out of his hand and ran with them held tightly against her breast to the window, where she stood with her back to him.

"When are you leaving for San Francisco and your rendezvous with Ted Kimball, Miss Thorndyke?"

Fern's only response to Sutton's question was a visible stiffening of her body.

"I take it the two of you set things up before you parted after the murder of Dade McGrath. You made plans to meet in San Francisco once things settled down some here, is that it? Where, Miss Thorndyke? Where exactly in San Francisco did you plan on hooking up with Ted Kimball?"

Fern spun around, the letter and its envelope still clutched in her hands. She nervously licked her lips and then, her voice so low that Sutton had trouble hearing her, said, "That money behind you on the dresser. There is nearly two hundred dollars there. Take it, Mr. Sutton. Take it and promise me that you won't try to find Ted Kimball. Take it and promise me that you'll leave both of us alone from now on so that we can live our lives together in peace. That's all we want. It isn't much by most standards. But to us, it's everything."

When Sutton didn't move, Fern, her lips quivering, asked, "Why don't you take the money? Isn't two hundred dollars enough? If it isn't, I'll try to get more. I *will* get more. Somehow I will."

"I don't want your money, Miss Thorndyke. I want the money the good people of Virginia City have offered to pay any man able to apprehend the killer of one of their own."

"If you'll give me enough time—one thousand dollars is a lot of money, Mr. Sutton—but I'll raise it. Ted and I will. Together we'll—"

"Where exactly is he in San Francisco?"

"Do you really think I would tell you that? So you could find him and bring him back here to stand trial—or maybe even kill him?" Fern began to laugh mirthlessly, her head thrown back, her eyes squeezed shut. A moment later her laughter suddenly died. She gave Sutton an angry look and pointed to the door. "Get out!"

He took a step toward her.

She stood her ground, her chin raised, a haughty expression that was tempered by barely hidden fear on her face. "Do you intend to hit me? Hurt me? *Force* me to tell you where Ted is? I warn you, Mr. Sutton, you can do your worst, but I shall never betray Ted."

"I just wanted to say that I do admire a woman who'll stand behind her man when the chips are down the way you're doing. I'm sorry that puts you and me at odds, but

that's the way the land lies, looks like. I'll be moseying on
now. Good day to you, Miss Thorndyke."

Before Sutton could open the door, Fern spoke his
name and he turned to face her.

"I want to warn you, Mr. Sutton," she said in a voice
that was both cold and passionate. "I'll do everything in
my power to keep you from getting to Ted Kimball. I'll
do everything and anything to stop you, so you had better watch your step from now on, Mr. Sutton. I've given
you fair warning."

"That's a downright decent thing of you to do, Miss
Thorndyke." He gave her a curt nod and then left the
room.

He made his way down into town, and when he
reached the stage depot, he inquired about the schedule
of stages going to San Francisco. He was told that there
was one stage per day heading west to San Francisco and
that it left at ten o'clock in the morning. He glanced at
the banjo clock on the wall of the depot. Twelve minutes
before ten o'clock. No time to even pack a carpetbag, he
thought. I'll be heading for San Francisco, looks like,
with only the clothes I'm standing up in. He sat down on
a wooden bench on the boardwalk outside the depot to
wait for Fern Thorndyke to appear.

By the time the stage pulled in at a few minutes after
ten o'clock, she had not appeared, and she had still not
appeared by the time the stage had been boarded by its
waiting passengers and pulled out again.

Tomorrow, Sutton told himself. She'll take tomorrow's
stage for sure, seeing as how she's no doubt in one hell of
a hurry to hook up again with Mr. Ted Kimball, who's
waiting on her way out there in San Francisco.

But Fern Thorndyke did not appear at the stage depot
the following morning to Sutton's great surprise and

greater dismay. He was about to return to the International Hotel, intending to try again the next day, when the uneasiness that had begun to grow within him goaded him, and instead of heading back to the hotel, he hurried up A Street toward the boardinghouse he had visited twice the day before.

This time, when he reached it, he found the woman who ran it seated in a rocking chair in the front yard, her fat face turned up to the sun, her eyes closed, and her hands folded across her chest.

He hurried past her but he had barely made it up the steps to the front porch when her voice boomed from behind him.

"Just one minute there!"

He turned. "I'm here to pay Miss Thorndyke a visit."

Before he could enter the house, the landlady was on her feet and waddling toward him. "You're here on a fool's errand, mister. There's nothing inside my house of any interest to you, so I'll thank you to turn around and take yourself off someplace else and stop bothering busy people such as myself."

"Miss Thorndyke—" Sutton began.

"She's gone," the landlady interrupted bluntly, planting her fisted hands on her flabby hips.

"Gone," Sutton repeated. "Gone where?"

"I don't know where she's gone nor do I care, since that woman's presence in my establishment was a stain on my professional reputation."

"What do you know then? When did she leave?"

"Yesterday it was that she paid her bill and marched pretty as you please, with her suitcase in hand, down the hill. But I'd no sooner heaved a sigh of relief than back she was, all upset about something, and paying me so that she could use her room one more night. Then she

writes a note and pays me to deliver it for her, which I
did.

"Well, sir, this morning she was up and out of here
bright and early, and he was waiting for her with a car-
riage and away the two of them drove. I expect that's the
last I'll see of her, which makes me not the least bit
sorry."

"Who was waiting for her?"

"Mr. Marcus Proctor himself, as big as life and twice
as arrogant. It was him she had me take that note to
yesterday. Oh, they make a pretty pair, those two do.
Both of them lying to the law the brazen way they did at
first to try to protect that fancy pants, Mr. Theodore
Kimball."

"Did Miss Thorndyke say anything to you by any
chance about taking a trip to San Francisco?"

"San Francisco? No, she did not. But, if she was heading for San Francisco, wouldn't you have thought she'd
have had the sense to take the stage instead of that car-
riage of Marcus Proctor's?"

She probably did plan to take the stage, Sutton
thought. But she must have spotted me yesterday down
at the depot lying in wait for her. She's smart enough to
have guessed I was intending to stick to her as tight as a
tick to a hound so she'd wind up leading me sooner or
later to Kimball. She must have made up her mind right
then and there to give me the slip. So she came on back
here, sent word to Proctor, and today he came and
helped her get past me. My guess is she's planning to
catch up with the stage and board it at Flat Rock, its first
stop west of Virginia City.

"If you're bent on catching up with that Thorndyke
woman," the landlady called out to Sutton as he left the

boardinghouse, "you'd do well to get yourself a real fast horse. She's got a headstart on you of at least two hours."

Sutton quickened his pace and then began to sprint down A Street, a plan already forming in his mind. I'll get my horse at the livery, he thought, after I stop by the hotel, and with any luck I ought to be able to catch up with Fern Thorndyke at Flat Rock Station, where she'll be spending tonight before setting out again on the stage for Frisco first thing tomorrow morning.

He stopped at the International Hotel and told the desk clerk to hold his room until he returned.

"I'll do that, Mr. Sutton, gladly. I'd been expecting your departure ever since I read the article in the paper this morning."

"Article? What article was that?"

"Why, this one right here, Mr. Sutton." The clerk handed Sutton a folded newspaper and pointed to a column headlined "Who's News." He scanned it, and as he did, so his name caught his eye:

> Mr. Lucas Sutton of this city informed ye editor yesterday that he is planning to embark on yet another manhunt. Readers of this newspaper are familiar with Mr. Sutton's recent manhunt as chronicled in this newspaper, so there is no need to recapitulate here the many dangers this brave and daring man encountered in his search for Mr. Vernon Adams, who had been taken captive by Apaches twenty years ago at the tender age of seven.
>
> This time Mr. Sutton intends to track down the infamous murderer of one of Virginia City's most notable citizens, Mr. Dade McGrath. We speak, of course, of the bloodthirsty Mr. Theodore Kimball, who in dastardly fashion did dispatch Mr. McGrath,

tearing him in a most untimely manner from this
vale of tears and leaving our community sorely be-
reaved. We wish Mr. Sutton much luck in his new
pursuit and hope that he will be successful in collect-
ing the thousand dollars in bounty money that has
been offered for the capture of the murderer of Mr.
Dade McGrath.

"I look forward, Mr. Sutton," said the desk clerk, "to
welcoming you back. I trust nothing untoward will happen to prevent you from returning to us."

"I appreciate your sentiments and I'll do my best to
stay out of the way of anything untoward. Now about
my clothes that I left to be laundered yesterday. Are
they—"

"They're waiting for you in your room, Mr. Sutton."

"Obliged for the fast service. Be seeing you."

Sutton made his way to his room, where he changed
clothes. He emerged from the room wearing faded jeans,
a blue flannel shirt, blue bandanna, buckskin jacket,
black slouch hat, and black army boots. Around his hips
he had strapped his cartridge belt, and hanging in its
oiled holster was his blunt-barreled sheriff's model Colt
.45.

He left the hotel and went to the livery stable, where
he told the farrier that he intended to bring his bill up to
date and that he wanted his horse. When the farrier had
brought him his bridled and saddled dun, he paid the
man for boarding and caring for the animal and then
swung into the saddle and rode out of the livery into the
bright sunshine of the warm April day.

As he abruptly wheeled his horse, intending to head
west out of town, a shot sounded, and he flinched as a
bullet whined its hot way past his right ear.

THREE

Sutton leapt from his saddle. He crouched for a moment behind his dun as he surveyed the street, the stores, the rooftops. And then he was running a zigzag course that took him from the street to the boardwalk and back to the street again. He dodged from one pillar supporting a store's overhang to the next one, drawing his revolver as he went, his eyes on the swarthy gunman with the full beard who was aiming at him from the far end of the street, where the man crouched behind a nearly empty wooden water trough.

Sutton halted in the doorway of a tin shop. Gripping the butt of his .45 in both hands and aiming at the man who had just tried to kill him, he yelled, "Throw down your gun! You don't and you're dead!"

Instead of obeying the shouted order, the man, whom Sutton was sure he had never seen before in his life, fired a second time. His bullet smashed into the jamb of the tin shop's door only inches away from Sutton's left shoulder. It splintered the wood and sent it spraying in every direction.

Sutton squeezed off a shot, but his target dropped down behind the trough and the shot went harmlessly over the man's head. Sutton sprinted forward, moving from doorway to doorway and ever closer to his would-be assassin, wondering two things as he went. Who? Why?

Who was the man who was trying to gun him down?
Why was the man trying to gun him down?

The man's head suddenly rose above the trough. As suddenly, so did his gun. He took aim at Sutton.

Sutton got off a swift snap shot that went wild. Behind him a woman cried out in alarm as she came out of a drugstore and then dashed back inside it. The street had emptied within minutes of the sound of the first shot, and Sutton, as he moved carefully closer to his target, heard the silence shrouding the area roaring in his ears. He put on a final burst of speed and ran forward, throwing himself down toward the water trough. He hit the ground hard and slid on his belly along it toward the end of the trough opposite the one where his target continued crouching.

He got to his knees and, bent over, got a grip on the end of the trough with his free left hand. He raised the wooden structure slightly, glad that it was less than half full of water, and then, straining, he managed to raise it still further. A moment later, putting his shoulder to the task, he upended the trough.

As the water poured from it to drench the gunman, who was spluttering and getting to his feet, Sutton overturned the trough.

It struck the bearded man as it fell, and he went down, dropping his six-gun as he did so.

Sutton sprang forward and seized a fistful of the downed man's shirt. He hauled him to his feet, placed the muzzle of his Colt against the man's forehead, and snarled, "Who the hell are you, mister, and why were you trying to ventilate me?"

The man's answer was a flung right fist which cracked sharply against Sutton's lower jaw, snapping his head backward and causing him to lose his grip on his attacker.

As the gunman turned to flee, Sutton reached out for him, but his fingers closed on empty air.

"Hold on!" Sutton roared, and sprinted after the man who was running down the street, his arms pumping at his sides as he glanced over his shoulder from time to time to see if he was being pursued.

Sutton bounded along in great strides, his heart pounding and his lungs on the verge of bursting. He veered when the man turned into a shadowy dead-end alley, and once inside the alley himself, he skidded to an abrupt halt and stood staring first in one direction, then in another, unable to believe that the man he had been after had apparently vanished.

When he made out the outline of a doorway in the dim light filtering down into the narrow alley, he headed for it and when he reached it, he pounded on it. He got no answer. He tried the door and found it unlocked. He opened it and peered into a small square room that was completely empty but, judging by its extensive shelving, might have served as a storage area for the mercantile up against which it abutted. He was about to close the door when he heard a sound behind him—a scraping sound. He quickly turned to find the man he had been after about to drop down from the square overhang above the door.

He grabbed his quarry's booted right foot with his left hand and yanked on it, causing the man to let out a blunt curse and come crashing down to the ground where he lay, groggily shaking his head and momentarily stunned because his head had struck the ground when he fell.

Sutton stood over him, his legs spread, his left hand twisted into a fist, his right thumb on the cocked sheriff's

Colt in his hand, which he leveled at the head of the gunman who had twice tried to kill him. "I'll ask you one more time," he said, his eyes drilling into those of the man lying on the ground by his boots. "Why'd you try to kill me?"

"Are *you* fixing to kill *me*, Sutton?"

"You know my name. How come you do? I've never laid so much as a single eye on you ever before in my life."

"You're a man with a reputation, Sutton. Lots of folks know your name. Folks you maybe don't know. You're a kind of local celebrity here in town, what with the way you've been spending your time trailing men for one reason or another."

"What's your grudge against me?" Sutton demanded.

"Nothing atall personal, Sutton." The man rose slowly to his feet. "Just a matter of business is all. Now let me ask you something. Would you gun down an unarmed man such as myself?"

Sutton knew he wouldn't, and he suspected that the man facing him and scratching his beard while he grinned with no merriment in his face or eyes knew it too. "What'd you mean when you said you threw down on me as a matter of business?"

"I'm not telling you nothing, Sutton. I'm being paid and paid good to kill you, not to answer your questions. Speaking of questions, what might you be fixing to do with me now, seeing as how you've got the upper hand here at the moment?"

"I'm taking you to Sheriff Hoskins and I'm going to see to it that he charges you with attempted murder. Now march yourself out of this alley, mister!"

The man, still grinning and still scratching, made a move to the right, turning away from Sutton as he did so.

Then, as Sutton moved forward to take up a position behind his prisoner, the man suddenly spun around, a snub-nosed .38 in his right hand.

Before the man could fire, Sutton's own six-gun thundered. The bearded man was thrown backward against the wall on the opposite side of the alley. Sutton watched through the thin haze of smoke rising from his gun barrel as the man clawed at the small red hole at the base of his throat while his mouth opened and he tried but failed to speak.

"Who hired you to do me in?" Sutton asked, hoping for an answer this time to his question but believing that the severely wounded man, even if he wanted to, was unable to give one.

The man Sutton had shot made a wet gurgling sound. Red saliva bubbled out from between his lips. He wiped them with the back of his right hand. Blinked. Sighed. Slid down the wall to the ground and died.

Sutton holstered his Colt, then went over to the dead man and patted his chest. He found the shoulder holster under the man's coat as he knew he would—the holster in which the would-be assassin had kept his hideout gun hidden.

He straightened and stood staring down at the man he had killed, gradually becoming aware as he did so of the sibilant whisperings that drifted toward him from the mouth of the alley. After taking one last look at the empty eyes of the man on the ground, Sutton turned and strode toward the entrance to the alley. As he neared it, the awed crowd who had gathered there parted to let him pass.

"We sent for the sheriff," Sutton heard someone say as he glanced at the faces of the men and the few women who made up the crowd and noted their expressions of awe and apprehension as they stared back at him.

"It was self-defense, sure enough," someone else added. "I saw what happened—how he drew on you so sneaky-like with that hideout gun of his."

Sutton once more scanned the faces of the crowd, wondering as he did so if he were looking for a trace of approval on the face of at least one of its members. He was about to head back to where he had left his dun when Sheriff Morley Hoskins arrived at the entrance to the alley. Sutton hooked his thumbs in his cartridge belt and, when Hoskins came up to him, said, "Morley, I had to do what I just did." He explained what he had done and why he had had to do it, concluding with, "I'd no intent to kill the man, but he forced my hand."

"Word was sent to me about what happened here," Hoskins declared soberly. "What got Bad Ed Kelvin out after you, Luke?"

Several members of the crowd leaned forward as if they wanted to be sure not to miss Sutton's answer to Hoskins' question.

"I can't answer that, Morley, on account of I just don't rightly know. Matter of fact, I never saw or even heard of that jasper—what'd you say his name was?—before."

"Ed Kelvin. Bad Ed Kelvin, he's called, and the name fits him. He's wanted in at least two territories and as many states that I know of, including right here in Nevada. He's been a gunhung rider of the long trails since long before God was born."

A man in the crowd snickered.

"Was his gun for hire?"

Hoskins nodded.

"Then I reckon somebody must have paid him to try to take me on account of there wasn't any quarrel or grudge

between Kelvin and me, at least not any I know of."
Sutton thoughtfully stroked his chin. "If I'm right in my
reckoning, I wouldn't be even the least bit surprised to
find I know who it was who set Kelvin on my back trail."

"Who do you think it was, Luke?"

"Can't say for sure, Morley, but my guess is that
maybe Kimball's fiancée—"

"Fern Thorndyke, you mean?"

Sutton nodded. "She warned me not to entertain any
notions of going after Kimball. The lady said she'd do
whatever it took to stop me from catching up with her
man." Sutton looked back at Kelvin's body.

"You think she hired Kelvin to kill you?" Hoskins
asked in a low voice.

"My suspicions lead me in her direction. I'd been keeping an eye on her the last couple of days and I found out
she was planning on making a trip to San Francisco. She
got a letter from there."

"From Kimball?"

"The letter wasn't signed, but my guess is it was from
him. Anyway, I figured she'd be heading there on the
stage so I staked out the depot, but she gave me the slip
with the help of Mr. Marcus Proctor. He called for her
early this morning and the two of them lit a shuck."

"For Frisco?"

"Maybe. Or maybe—and this is the number I'll bet my
poke on—Proctor's taking her to Flat Rock so she can
board the stage there. I was heading for Flat Rock when"
—Sutton pointed at Kelvin—"that wolf started standing
in my way."

"Well, he won't be standing in your way—or anyone
else's neither—now," Hoskins observed.

"Be seeing you, Morley."

"You take care now, Luke."

Sutton returned to where he had left his horse. He swung into the saddle, wheeled the animal, slammed his heels into its flanks, and went galloping west.

Virginia City was behind him and he was riding along the narrow stage road when he first became aware that there was another rider some distance behind him. He cantered on, the dun beneath him picking its way among frost-cracked boulders of varying sizes, glancing over his shoulder from time to time.

When he saw that the rider on his back trail was gaining on him, he hit the flanks of his dun hard with both booted heels, and then as his horse moved forward in an abrupt burst of speed, he turned the animal, left the stage road, and guided the dun down a sloping grade of broken shale and into a stand of tall pin oaks. Once hidden from sight by the trees, he turned his horse again and rode back the way he had come on a course parallel with his earlier trail. He kept his eyes turned to the north, and only minutes passed before he spotted the man who had been riding his back trail.

He drew rein and sat his saddle, watching the stranger as the man continued heading west along the stage road. He sits real tall in the saddle, Sutton thought. Rangy fellow. But dressed in what looks like to me to be his Sunday-go-to-meeting duds. Black coat of clean broadcloth. Purple shirt with a white paper collar and black tie. Striped trousers. Shiny high-topped black shoes. No hat.

No hat? Riding hard under a hot sun with no hat? The man most likely's not a tried and true trailsman, all things considered, Sutton decided. Too duded up. Hatless. Wearing townsman's shoes instead of boots. And he's far too citified-looking to be a granger riding out to see the scenery of a spring afternoon.

Sutton, his hands gripping his reins and folded around his saddle horn, watched from behind an oak as the man slowed and then halted the dapple he was riding. He watched him look around, reconnoitering the area, and then use a hand to shield his eyes from the sun as he stared west. When the man stood up in his stirrups, still peering west, Sutton made his move. He heeled his dun's flanks and went galloping north toward the rider, who, when he heard Sutton coming, turned in his saddle and waved, a smile brightening his pale face.

Sutton rode on and then drew rein as he reached the stage road and the other rider, wondering as he did so why the stranger's face seemed vaguely familiar to him since he could not recall ever having seen or met him before. With his hand resting on the butt of his .45, he asked in a stern voice, "How come you were following me, mister?"

"Well, this is lonely country," the man answered amiably, "and when I caught a glimpse of you up ahead of me, I decided to try to catch up with you in the hope that, since we were both traveling in the same direction, we could do so together for a while and keep each other company."

"Where you headed?"

"My brother has a small ranch west of here. It's in the foothills of the Sierra Nevada. I say, sir. I do hope I've not angered or annoyed you by trying to join you in your journey. If I have unwittingly done so, I humbly beg your pardon."

The face of Bad Ed Kelvin flickered in Sutton's mind. His hand remained on the butt of his six-gun.

"I'll wait here until you've gone ahead if that is your

pleasure, sir," the rider facing Sutton volunteered. "Though I hope you will let me ride with you. Two men together in this wilderness are better than one man alone. One can never tell what dangers lurk along the trail."

"What's your name?"

"Bryan Lenton." The man held out his hand.

Sutton ignored it. He moved his horse out, indicating with a curt nod that Lenton could join him if he so desired.

Lenton did, and the two men rode together for some time without speaking. But at last Lenton broke the silence by asking, "Where are you headed, Mr.—"

"Name's Sutton. I'm headed west."

"To any place in particular, if I may be so bold as to inquire?"

"San Francisco."

"Ah yes, San Francisco. I've been there several times on business. On pleasure too, I might add. In that marvelous city by the sea—it's a magical place, Mr. Sutton. Why, out there in San Francisco one can readily make oneself believe that gold and lovely ladies are both lying about in the hot sunshine just waiting for an enterprising man to come and claim them."

Sutton gave Lenton a sidelong glance. Where and when had he seen the man before? He could not recall, and his failure made him uneasy since he was keenly aware that trail-met strangers can be a man's foe for any one of a multitude of reasons while masquerading as his friend.

"Mr. Sutton, I could give you the names of some business associates of mine in San Francisco. They would be, I am quite certain, more than happy to welcome you to their city and to offer you any assistance you might need to successfully complete whatever business you plan to engage in while on the coast."

"Nice of you to offer to help me out, Lenton, but your business associates—they'd most likely not be able to help me out in the kind of business I'm planning on taking care of out there in San Francisco."

Sutton rode on, swaying slightly in the saddle as his dun moved over uneven and upward-sloping ground. Ahead of him in the distance, the Sierra Nevada loomed black and brightly snowcapped. Around him sycamores and birch trees grew and to the south a stream ran, its surface slicked by the sun, its banks lined with cottonwoods. The air began to grow cooler as Sutton, with Lenton at his side, rode higher up into the foothills.

"Where do you plan to make camp for the night, Mr. Sutton?"

Lenton's voice shattered Sutton's vision of the blue-eyed and honey-haired Fern Thorndyke. "Don't plan to."

"But—"

"Lenton, we're getting into high country. Does your brother herd clouds or cows?"

"My brother?" Lenton frowned and then, brightening, continued, "Oh yes, my brother. Very amusing, Mr. Sutton. Clouds or cows. Yes, highly amusing."

"Most ranchers, they prefer level land to build on and use any high country that might happen to be in their neighborhood for summer pasture."

"I'm not really very familiar with the ways of ranchers, I'm afraid." Lenton coughed. His hand rose to cover his mouth. And then it slid beneath his coat. When it reappeared a moment later, it held a Smith & Wesson .44. "But I am familiar with the ways of bounty hunters, Sutton."

Sutton's impulse was to go for his gun, but he knew that if he did, Lenton would probably fire before he could even unleather his Colt. When Lenton gestured, a deceptively casual movement made with his gun hand, Sutton reluctantly raised his hands high above his head.

"What kind of a hand is this you're playing Lenton?" Sutton asked, intently studying the man's pale face that was made paler by his inky eyes and their black-lashed lids and eyebrows. He was clean-shaven except for sideburns which came down below his ear lobes before curving sharply out upon his cheeks. His hair, black but shot with streaks of gray at the temples, was cropped close to his head.

Lenton chuckled and then answered Sutton's question. "You ask what kind of hand I'm playing? A winning hand, Sutton. A hand full of high cards."

"You've got the advantage on me, Lenton, since you know me and I don't know you from a ring-tailed raccoon. Who exactly are you and what've you got against me that's put that gun in your hand and got it aiming right at my brisket?"

"I've been reading about you in Virginia City's *Territorial Enterprise,*" Lenton declared with a trace of a sneer. "The first time was when you won that marksman's shooting contest down in Carson City a while ago. I must say that the photograph of you that accompanied that article about the contest you won didn't do you justice, Sutton. In person, you're much leaner and brighter-eyed than you seemed to be in that picture.

"At any rate, that was the first time your name came to my attention. At the time, I never dreamed that one day our trails would cross but, as you can see, cross they have." Lenton's eyes narrowed to black slivers. "The next time I read about you—it was Dan DeQuille's rather melodramatic account of how you helped to settle the Comstock miners' strike. But the most recent time that I read about you proved to be of significance to me. That was only yesterday—in the *Enterprise*'s 'Who's News' column. I learned that you intended to try to collect the bounty offered for the apprehension of Theodore Kimball."

Sutton watched Lenton's eyes widen and the man's face assume an exaggerated expression of distress.

"I couldn't allow that, Sutton."

"Why not?"

Lenton held up a hand, his head cocked to one side. "Let me explain in my own way and in my own good time." He drew a deep breath. "I began to follow you, Sutton. More than once I thought I saw my chance to kill you."

Sutton stiffened.

"But something always interfered. A passerby. Your sudden change of direction. But then today, when that outlaw Kelvin tried to shoot you, I thought my troubles were over. I thought someone else was about to do the job for me, but it was not to be, unfortunately for me."

Sutton, staring unblinkingly at Lenton's face, suddenly remembered where he had seen the man. Lenton had been in the crowd that had gathered at the mouth of the alley after he had shot and killed Kelvin. "You were there right after the shooting," Sutton stated. "In the crowd. I remember seeing you there."

"That's true. And I was fortunate enough to have heard what you said to Sheriff Hoskins about Miss Thorndyke and her patron, Mr. Proctor. I heard you tell Hoskins that you intended to try to catch up with that pair at the stage station at Flat Rock. Well, to shorten a long and somewhat tedious story, Sutton, I followed you out of town—and here the two of us are."

"You said before you were bent on seeing to it that I didn't get to collect the Kimball bounty money. How come, Lenton? What's your stake in that matter?"

"Let me answer your questions this way, Sutton—by first saying that my name is not Lenton. It is Lorne Mc-Grath."

Sutton's breath, which he had not realized he had been holding, sighed sibilantly out from between his lips as understanding came to him. "Bill Wright told me Dade McGrath had a brother—"

"Now perhaps you can guess why I had to stop you from going after Kimball, Sutton."

"On account of you've decided to go after him yourself and you don't want me or anybody else getting in your way."

"That is correct, since I now believe I know where Kimball can be found. But it is not the bounty money that motivates me, Sutton; let me hasten to assure you of that fact. It is revenge that drives me. I intend to see to it that my brother's murder is avenged."

Five ghosts suddenly swooped down upon Sutton, gibbering, gesticulating. Among them was his bright-eyed brother Dan, who had been killed by the other four ghosts now circling him in Sutton's mind, the four remnants of the men Sutton had stalked, found, and then seen their lives end. There's a word for what's happening here, he thought. McGrath's out to do what I once did and that sure is—he hunted for the word he wanted and found it—ironic. This whole thing's as ironic as hell celebrating Christmas'd be.

"You can see now why I have to kill you, Sutton," McGrath stated tonelessly. "And when I have done so, I

will ride on to Flat Rock Station and, if your theory as
expressed to Sheriff Hoskins is correct, Miss Thorndyke
will lead me to her lover in San Francisco—to the man
who murdered my brother!"

Sutton's eyes dropped to McGrath's right index finger
that was slowly squeezing the trigger of the revolver he
held in his hand. Then, an instant before McGrath fired,
Sutton swiftly swung his right leg over his horse's neck
and as swiftly slid out of the saddle. He hit the ground
only a moment before McGrath's shot sailed harmlessly
above the back of the dun. Sutton crouched and went
under the belly of his horse. As he came up on its other
side, his right hand shot up and he seized the wrist of
McGrath's gun hand. He gave it a sharp twist, squeezing
it at the same time, and McGrath, despite his struggles to
free himself, was first forced to drop his revolver and
then to slide out of his saddle.

Sutton threw him to the ground and, at the same time,
kicked McGrath's gun out of the fallen man's reach. Mc-
Grath rolled over and clawed with his free hand at Sutton's hand, which still gripped his wrist. Sutton let go of
McGrath and bent down, intending to haul the man to
his feet. But as he was about to do so, McGrath suddenly
struck out with one foot and savagely kicked Sutton's left
shin. Pain sped through Sutton's leg and up into his pel-
vis, sharp and shattering. As Sutton staggered backward
on his injured leg, McGrath leaped to his feet and lashed
out with both fists, his left one landing on Sutton's right
bicep, his right one flying harmlessly past Sutton's
quickly averted face.

Sutton threw a hard right and heard with grim satisfaction the *crick* as his knuckles made contact with Mc-
Grath's lower jaw. He gave the man a left jab and then a
right uppercut that snapped McGrath's head backward,

almost toppling the man. But McGrath, swearing now and beginning to sweat, landed a series of body blows that sent Sutton reeling backward to fall over a rotting deadfall that lay on the ground directly behind him.

Before he could rise, McGrath flew forward and threw himself bodily upon Sutton. They battled, each man pummeling the other with his fists, locked together and rolling first one way and then the other like some bizarre organism bent on destroying itself. McGrath reached out, seized a rock, raised it.

Sutton's left fist knocked it out of McGrath's hand. At the same time, he kneed McGrath in the gut and, when the man gasped for air and doubled over, he seized his opponent by the neck and, holding tightly to him with both hands, began to squeeze as hard as he could.

McGrath gagged. His eyes began to bulge. His tongue burst from between parted lips. He tore at Sutton's fingers with all ten of his own.

Sutton's grip held firm as he watched McGrath's eyes. When he saw them begin to glaze as McGrath started to slip into unconsciousness, he tightened his grip on the man's neck. Then, as McGrath's body abruptly went limp, Sutton released him, shoved him to one side, and got shakily to his feet, where he stood staring down at the second man who had tried to kill him in the course of a single day.

Sutton's breath came in short sharp gasps. He flexed his fingers, feeling the sharp aches in them that were the result of the blows he had given McGrath. He reached for his gun.

But before Sutton's Colt could clear leather, McGrath regained consciousness. His hand snaked swiftly out and seized Sutton's left ankle. As Sutton tried to free himself, McGrath grabbed his other ankle and jerked on both of

them, sending Sutton crashing down to the ground. Mc-
Grath leaped on top of him, and his hands circled Sutton's throat and began to squeeze.

Now it was Sutton's turn to claw at his attacker's
strong hands, but he could not break McGrath's grip on
him. He tried desperately to suck air into his lungs, but
he could not do so. Above him the world began to blur.
McGrath suddenly sprouted four—then six—eyes. The
sun spun in the bright blue sky, a gold coin flipped into a
distant sea. Spittle slipped from between McGrath's lips
and fell on Sutton's face that was already wet with sweat.
Sutton, desperate because he could not breathe and because he felt himself sinking into a hazy red world where
nothing was recognizable and everything was painful,
managed to draw his six-gun. He raised it and struck
McGrath on the side of the head with the gun's barrel.

McGrath was knocked to one side by the blow. He fell
heavily to the ground and lay there moaning, his fingers
convulsing, his entire body twitching.

Sutton once again got to his feet and stood there unsteadily, staring down at McGrath.

McGrath looked up, wide-eyed, and then sat up, his
fingers scrabbling along the ground as he searched for a
stick, a stone—any weapon he could use against the man
who was towering over him and whose gun might at any
minute spit death in his direction.

Sutton, his chest heaving, swallowed several times until the dryness of his mouth and throat was almost gone.
When he spoke, his voice was harsh, rasping. "Back up,
McGrath, till you're up against that oak over there behind you."

McGrath stared wordlessly at Sutton for a long moment before beginning to obey the order. But he had
eased along the ground for only a matter of inches when

he threw himself forward and started to rise, his hands reaching out for Sutton.

Sutton's outthrust right boot caught McGrath in the middle of the chest. The blow knocked the air from McGrath's lungs and he went down again.

Sutton repeated his order and this time McGrath obeyed it.

As McGrath on his buttocks slid along the ground, Sutton backed toward his dun, keeping his gun on McGrath, and removed a coil of rope that hung from his saddle horn. He strode over to McGrath, who sat silent and sullen with his back braced against the towering oak tree to which Sutton had directed him.

"Put your hands around behind the tree," Sutton barked, and when McGrath had slowly and with obvious reluctance circled the tree with his arms, Sutton went behind the tree and quickly tied McGrath's wrists together. When he judged that the knots he had made were sufficient and secure, he pulled his bowie knife from his boot and severed the rope. As he rounded the tree again, McGrath looked up at him. "Are you going to kill me?"

Sutton shook his head.

"Torture me?"

Sutton shook his head again.

"Then—what?"

Instead of answering, Sutton went to his dun, hung what remained of his rope on his saddle horn, booted a stirrup, and swung into the leather.

"You—you're going to leave me here? You can't leave me here. Not like this, you can't. I'll starve—die of thirst. Sutton, you can't—"

"I can, McGrath. And I am going to leave you right where you are the way you are. Maybe you'll get lucky.

Maybe somebody'll come along and let you loose—before anything bad has a chance to happen to you."

"Shoot me! A quick death would be better than—"

"I've already killed one man today, McGrath. I didn't relish having to do that deed. I'm not a man who savors killing other men. The way you are—well, you've got a chance to maybe survive. With a little bit of luck."

"If I do," McGrath muttered savagely, his black eyes blazing as he stared up at Sutton, "I'll get you, Sutton. As sure as the sun sits up there in the sky right this minute, I'll get you for this!"

Sutton ignored the hatred flaring in McGrath's eyes. He picked up his reins, booted the flanks of his dun, and rode away with McGrath's curses echoing in his ears.

FOUR

It was dusk when Sutton rode into the combination stage stop and road ranch at Flat Rock. He dismounted and tethered his dun to one of the poles of the corral that held close to a dozen horses. Turning, he made his way to the building that stood not far away, glancing at the wagon and team that stood near it, and pausing as he passed the stage to glance into its empty interior.

Once inside the building, he stood with his back almost touching the door he had closed behind him, his hand on the butt of his six-gun, his eyes quickly becoming accustomed to the wavering yellow light of the coal-oil lamps that lighted the huge room in which he found himself.

His lips compressed themselves into a thin grim line as he stared at Fern Thorndyke and Marcus Proctor, who were seated together at a table in the rear of the room. He started toward them, but before he had reached their table, Fern happened to glance his way. She gasped and almost dropped the tin cup she was raising to her lips. She put it down and her hand snaked across the table and came to rest on Proctor's forearm.

"Evening, Miss Thorndyke," Sutton greeted her pleasantly as he arrived at their table. "You too, Proctor."

Proctor blanched. He exchanged startled glances with Fern.

"I don't usually light 'less I'm asked to, but this time's

different," Sutton said and sat down. "This time I reckon
you'd be likely to tell me to hightail it to Hades were I to
ask permission to join you two." He tilted his hat back on
his head and hooked his thumbs in his cartridge belt.
"Spring's a nice time of year to take a trip," he commented. "Especially to San Francisco. Air's clear as a bell
up in the Sierras. And out in Frisco it's not yet too hot."

"How did you—" Fern's voice trailed away.

"How did I find you?" Sutton asked. "It was easy."

"Go away, Mr. Sutton," Fern said in a decidedly shaky
voice. "Leave us alone."

Ignoring her order, he turned his attention to Proctor
and asked, "Are you also planning on paying Ted Kimball a visit out in San Francisco, Proctor, or are you heading back home to Virginia City now that you've brought
Miss Thorndyke this far?"

"That's none of your damned business!" Proctor
snapped indignantly. "And you heard the lady's request,
Sutton. So I'd be obliged to you if you'd honor it and
leave us alone."

"Yes, sir?" The man who had materialized at the table
next to Sutton's elbow wore a greasy gray apron that had
once been white. "I'm Charlie Easton, this place's proprietor. You hungry? Looking for lodgings?"

"I'm both," Sutton answered. "I'm—"

"What say?" Easton cupped a hand behind his ear.

Sutton, speaking more loudly, declared, "I'm both. I'm
hungry and I'm looking for lodgings." He glanced at the
small square blackboard of the kind used by children in
school which hung on the wall and on which someone
had chalked the menu offered at the stage stop. "I'll have
—" As the proprietor's hand again went behind his ear,
Sutton raised his voice. *"I'll have a steak, real rare. Fried*

potatoes with onions. Baked beans. Coffee. And a room for the night."

"The food's no problem. But as for a room—well, the fact is, we're full up. But if you're amenable and so's one of my other lodgers, you could share a bed. And," he added with a wink, "save yourself some money by doing just that."

Sutton, not at all pleased by the prospect offered by Easton, frowned. "That's the best—"

Easton cupped his ear in his hand, leaned down toward Sutton, and said, "Speak up, son."

"That's the best you can do for me, is it?"

"That's it, mister."

Sutton reluctantly nodded his assent to the proposal, and Easton promptly disappeared.

When he returned some time later, bearing the meal Sutton had ordered, to the table Sutton was sharing in silence with Fern and Proctor, he pointed to a burly man wearing a full beard who was seated by himself in a corner of the room near the door.

"That fellow over there, his name's Carter. He's traveling on the stage to Frisco. I spoke to him, and he says he don't mind saving some money. He says you're welcome to share his bed. He's in room two. The bed'll cost you a buck fifty apiece. Your meal's a dollar even."

Sutton paid the man and began to eat. He was forking a piece of bleeding beefsteak into his mouth when Fern suddenly rose to her feet and left the table. Proctor followed her. Sutton turned his head slightly and saw them take seats at a distant table next to Carter's.

Later, when he finished his meal, he got up and went over to speak to Carter. "Name's Sutton, Carter. Seems like you and me, we'll be bunking together tonight."

As the two men shook hands, Carter smiled and said, "I think I should warn you, Mr. Sutton."

Sutton's eyes narrowed. "Warn me? About what?"

"I snore."

"So do I sometimes, Carter, so I reckon that means we come out even."

Sutton accepted Carter's invitation to sit in on a poker game Carter had organized earlier, and he won the first pot and then lost the next two. Carter, he noticed, lost all three, but it was obvious that the man was not ready to give up. When the clock on the wall read midnight, Sutton withdrew from the game, bade good night to Fern and Proctor, who pointedly ignored him, and went in search of room number two which was located, he soon discovered, on the second floor of the building.

Once inside it, he lit a coal-oil lamp, pleased to see that the room's single window was not much wider than an old-fashioned fort's loophole. But he was not pleased to see that the door had no lock on it. Nobody can climb in that skinny window after me, he thought. He locked the window's wooden shutters. And now, he thought, nobody can climb up a ladder and try poking a gun at me through that window. But that door's another matter. He picked up one of the chairs that the room contained and propped it under the door's knob.

Carter, he thought. When—if—he ever comes to bed, he'll have to rouse me to let him in, which might not make him altogether happy, but at least what I did to that door'll keep me secure enough in the meantime.

He unstrapped his cartridge belt, took off his hat, and placed them both on a small table that stood next to the bed. He sat down on the lumpy tick that was, he thought, judging by its strong smell, probably stuffed with straw gone sour, and pulled off his boots. Then he blew out the lamp and lay down on his back on the bed. He closed his eyes and saw an evil-eyed image of Bad Ed Kelvin crouching in the darkness behind his eyelids. It was replaced almost immediately by an image nearly as ugly— that of Marcus Proctor. Then sleep banished the image of Proctor as it claimed Sutton.

He was adrift in a dream of an elusive wild horse he had stalked unsuccessfully through timbered mountains and city streets when he awoke with a start because someone was pounding on the door and shouting his name loud enough, he thought, to wake everyone for miles around.

Carter, he thought as he got up, removed the chair he had used to block the door, and opened it. Carter brushed past him into the room that was faintly illuminated by the new day's first light, which was seeping through the cracks in the window's wooden shutter.

"What the hell do you think you're doing, locking me out of my own room!" he roared at Sutton.

A moment later a coal-oil lamp Carter had lit flickered into bright yellow life.

"I didn't want to have to entertain any unwelcome guests," Sutton replied. "There's no lock on the door." Turning away from Carter, he was about to replace the chair under the door's knob when he heard swift movement behind him. He let go of the chair and started to turn— He caught only the briefest glimpse of the gun in Carter's hand, which he was holding by the barrel, before the heavy iron slammed down against his skull and he staggered backward, his vision beginning to blur.

Carter struck him a second time and Sutton felt himself going down. He reached out for something to hold on to, but there was nothing within reach. He fell into a void that was as deep as it was dark, a black void where consciousness of himself and of the world around him were abruptly torn from him.

He regained consciousness in slow sluggish stages, gradually becoming aware of the fact that he was hatless, bootless, and gunless, as he had been before his encounter with Carter.

Groggy, he opened his eyes to see thin shafts of sunlight streaming through cracks in wooden walls. He swore when he realized that he had been gagged and his hands and ankles were tightly bound with rope. He was lying on his left side, his hands tied behind his back, his face half-buried in dusty straw. Every move he made, even the slightest, caused pain to seize and squeeze his skull.

A barn, he thought. And I'm up in its hayloft. But what barn? And where's it at? The stage station? Someplace else? He had no way of knowing. He strained at the ropes binding his wrists and ankles, but they stayed firmly in place. He turned his head and rubbed his face against his shoulder, trying but failing to dislodge the gag which was held in place by a strip of cloth tied around his head.

Sweat broke out on his face. It poured into his eyes, stinging them. He shut them and then opened them again, lying still, looking around. There was a pitchfork sprouting from a huge pile of hay not far away. Bales of hay bound with wire were stacked in a tall pile against one wall. In the wall behind him was a door, closed now, through which the bales could be hauled up into the loft.

He gave up his efforts and concentrated on the simple act of breathing. Dust was clogging his nostrils, and the gag in his mouth seemed about to choke him. Got to think this thing through, he told himself. It's no use me flopping around on the floor like a trussed-up pig. Got to find some way to get loose. But how?

He silently swore as he thought of Carter. How come Carter went for me, he wondered. I never even saw the man before tonight.

He rolled over and then rolled over again, making his way toward the nearest wall. When he was lying on his side next to it, he raised his booted feet and slammed his heels into the wall, making a resounding noise. He repeated the action several times in swift succession and then, breathing hard from the exertion the effort had caused him, he lay still and waited to see if the noise he had made would elicit a response.

It didn't.

He repeated his action, slamming his booted feet even harder against the wooden wall. The muscles in his thighs and calves began to ache from the effort, but he kept it up.

Still no response.

Where's Easton, he wondered as he at last lay still again, fighting for breath. He tried one more time to rouse the road ranch's proprietor, and when his efforts failed to bear fruit, he gave up and turned his attention elsewhere. His eyes roved about the loft, falling on its closed outer door. The pitchfork. The barren walls. The bales of hay. He stared thoughtfully at the bales for a long moment and then began to inch his way across the floor toward them.

When he reached them, he got up on his knees and began to examine them, shouldering unsuitable ones out of his way. He had tumbled several bales to the floor before he found one that he believed would serve his purpose. One of the strands of baling wire that bound it ended in a twist where the wire's two ends met. Two sharp lengths of wire jutted jaggedly upward from the twist.

Sutton turned, placed his back to the bale, brought his hands up as far as he could—and found he couldn't reach the two protruding ends of the wire. He got unsteadily to his feet and then, hunkering down, he managed to bring the rope that bound his hands into contact with the ends of the wire. He moved his hands up and down, stopping from time to time to straighten the jagged ends of wire with his blindly groping fingers.

It was a long and tedious process, but he kept at it and he kept hoping. He could not see whether his efforts were effective. Still, he kept at it, his hands moving up and down in a kind of seesaw motion. After what seemed to him hours of effort, he felt a loose strand of rope touch the back of his left hand.

It's fraying, he thought. He continued his struggle to free himself, and after another eternity had passed, he let out a whoop of delight as he felt the rope finally give way. He shook the frayed remains of it from his hands and then reached up and tore the wet gag from his mouth. Minutes later, he had the rope off his ankles.

Tossing it aside, he went to the opening in the loft and looked down at the ladder lying on the floor of the barn below. Whoever put me up here, he thought, didn't mean for me to get down from here in any easy way. He spun around, picked up several bales of hay, and tossed them down to the floor below. Then, crouching, he leaped through the opening in the loft's floor to land safely on the bales. He was up in an instant and sprinting out of the barn.

Once inside the empty road ranch, he let out a wordless yell. When it got no response, he headed for the kitchen. Deserted. He bounded up the stairs to the second floor and began opening the doors of empty rooms. He found Easton behind the fourth one he opened. The man was asleep in a dingy room that wasn't much larger than a cubbyhole. He went over to the bed and shook him awake.

"What—who—mister, what the hell do you think you're doing?" Easton, who was wearing a flannel nightcap and nightgown, spluttered as he stared fearfully up at Sutton.

"How come you didn't answer me when I was making that unholy ruckus up in your loft by pounding my boot heels against the wall?" Sutton roared.

"What ruckus?" Easton whined. "I didn't hear no racket—but then I'm somewhat hard of hearing." He pointed to an ear trumpet lying on the table next to the bed and gave Sutton a sickly grin. "Don't like to use that blasted thing in public. Vanity of vanities, you understand." He gave Sutton a suspicious squint. "You say you were raising a ruckus up in my hayloft? What for were you?"

Sutton answered the question and then, by shouting questions of his own, he learned from Easton that Fern Thorndyke, Marcus Proctor, and the man named Carter had all departed with the rest of the passengers on the stage for San Francisco at first light that morning. A good seven hours or more ago, according to Easton.

"Proctor and Carter seemed to me to be chums by that time," Easton volunteered, and when Sutton asked him what he meant, he stated that he had seen money change hands between the two men in the wee hours of the morning after everyone else had gone to bed.

"The money—it went from whose hand to whose?" Sutton barked.

"From Proctor's into Carter's." Easton paused a moment and then, slyly: "You thinking the same thing I'm thinking?"

"I am if you're thinking that Proctor paid Carter to knock me out and toss me all trussed up into your hayloft. When's the next stage for San Francisco due?"

"Not till day after tomorrow."

"There's none tomorrow?" Sutton asked, forgetting to shout.

Easton reached for his trumpet and thrust the small end of it into his right ear. "Eh?"

Sutton repeated his question and was reminded by Easton that the next day was Sunday.

"There ain't no westbound stage—eastbound either—on the Lord's day," Easton declared piously. Then, with a grin: "I get to have me a day of rest come Sunday."

Sutton dug a dollar from his pocket and tossed it on the bed.

"What's this for?" Easton asked him.

"Feed for my horse." Sutton turned on his heels and left the room, not caring whether or not the proprietor had heard him and knowing that he would not wait for the stage to arrive two days hence even though he had little hope of overtaking the stage, which had a seven-hour headstart on him. He made his way to the room he was to have shared the night before with Carter. There he was relieved to find his cartridge belt and gun, his boots and his hat. He put them on and then left the road ranch.

He freed his dun, which still stood tethered to the corral post where he had left the animal the day before, and led it into the barn. He watered the horse sparingly and then grained it. While the dun was eating, he stripped his gear from it, shook out his saddle blanket, and rubbed the horse down with a clean piece of muslin he found hanging from a nail.

Later, after getting the dun ready to ride, he led it from the barn, swung into the saddle, and rode away from the road ranch, heading west toward the snow-capped ranges of the Sierra Nevada, and San Francisco, which lay beyond them.

After sleeping for nearly thirteen hours straight following his arrival in San Francisco, Sutton awoke in the room he had rented in the Sailors' Haven Hotel, dressed, strapped his cartridge belt around his lean hips, and ate an enormous meal in the hotel's somewhat seedy dining room. Then, after consulting the piece of paper on which he had written the address of Ted Kimball's law office, which Marcus Proctor had given him during their first meeting, he made his way to Commercial Street. He found number 52 to be an unimposing four-story brick building. After checking the building's directory, he made his way to the third floor and knocked on the door that bore a scripted message in black paint: Theodore Kimball, Attorney at Law.

He knocked, waited, and when no one answered the door, he knocked again, louder this time, and then, when he again failed to elicit a response, he tried the door and found it locked. He turned and knocked on the door opposite Kimball's office, which bore a plaque identifying itself as Moss & Sons, Ship Chandlers. When a cheerful female voice called out, "Come in!" he entered the office, took off his hat, and asked the young woman seated at a desk behind a wooden railing if she could give him any information concerning the whereabouts of Mr. Kimball, her next door neighbor.

"Oh, I'm afraid I can't help you on that score, sir," she

replied. "I've not seen Mr. Kimball in ever so long—none of us here at Moss and Sons has."

"How long has it been since you've seen him?"

"Well—" The woman put a finger to her chin and stared at the ceiling. "Mr. Kimball paid a visit to Virginia City, and he hasn't been seen by anyone in the building, as far as I know, since his departure from San Francisco."

Sutton thanked the woman and turned to go.

"I'm terribly sorry I couldn't be more helpful, sir. Perhaps you should talk to the building's janitor. His name's Mr. Cushman and he has living quarters in the basement."

"I'm obliged to you. I'll do that."

Sutton found Cushman in a one-room hovel behind the boiler in the basement of the building. He introduced himself and told the janitor that he was interested in locating Mr. Theodore Kimball.

Cushman gave Sutton a speculative stare. "What's your business with Mr. Kimball?"

"It's private and none of yours," Sutton snapped, angered by the janitor's undisguised insolence. But then, deciding that anger was not an asset to him in this particular situation, he forced himself to smile. He thrust a hand into his pocket and it emerged holding an eagle. "I imagine a keen-eyed man such as yourself keeps pretty close tabs on his tenants' comings and goings." The eagle wound up in Cushman's vest pocket.

The money melted the man. "I've not laid eyes on Mr. Kimball since he left for Virginia City almost a month ago. But it seems lots of people are looking for him, including that policeman that's posted across the street from this building."

"Policeman?"

"He's on the lookout for Mr. Kimball, he told me when

he came nosing around here asking everybody in the building questions about Mr. Kimball. He said the law in Virginia City let the law here know that Mr. Kimball's a wanted man, so they put a man on this building and one at the place where Kimball lives—or lived. What's he done, do you know?"

"Who else besides me and the policeman you just mentioned have been looking for Kimball?"

"A man and a woman."

Sutton described Fern Thorndyke and Marcus Proctor to Cushman.

"That's them. They both seemed real anxious to find Mr. Kimball. Same as you and the police seem to be."

"What else can you tell me about Mr. Kimball? What kind of clients did he do business with? Did he keep regular business hours? I'd like to know anything you might have noticed about him that could turn out to be helpful to me in trying to track him down."

Cushman eased the eagle out of his vest pocket. He looked lustfully at it and then at Sutton. He returned it to his vest pocket, his eyes boldly meeting Sutton's. When another of Sutton's eagles had joined the first in Cushman's vest pocket, the janitor volunteered: "The only other thing I know for sure about Mr. Kimball is that he represented Miss Roberta Pritchard—free of charge. How I happen to know is, I was taking out the trash from Mr. Kimball's office one night and he was working late, and she came to see him and said she was in trouble with the law again but she had little money for a lawyer, and he told her after he'd heard her out not to fret because he'd take her case free of charge."

Cushman guffawed and winked at Sutton. "Now a man might conclude from what Mr. Kimball did for Miss Pritchard that he had a big heart. Well, maybe he did, to give the devil his due. But the fact is Miss Pritchard is a real trim-figured and not the least bit ugly lady—if you take my meaning." Cushman grinned, revealing a shiny gold tooth.

Sutton, his interest piqued by Cushman's tale, asked, "Who's this Miss Roberta Pritchard?"

"She's a missionary. She runs a home for young Chinese girls who've been bought over in China and then shipped here and put to work in the cribs and parlor houses like those over on Jackson Street in Chinatown. She's been in trouble with the law, Miss Pritchard has. The slavers—"

"Slavers?"

"The men who buy the girls in China and sell them once they've got them shipped over here—they've hauled Miss Pritchard into court on charges of abducting their women. That's why she came to Mr. Kimball for help. If you ask me, she and women like her ought to stick to their knitting and not go meddling in matters that's none of their business. Hell, those Chinese girls—they *like* what they're doing, and they do it real good too, I can tell you for true. You ought to try one or two of them out, mister."

"Where might I find Miss Pritchard?" Sutton asked, slightly sickened by the lecherous glint in Cushman's eyes and the way the janitor was avidly licking his thick lips.

Cushman gave Sutton an address on Dupont Street in Chinatown and Sutton told the janitor that he was staying at the Sailors' Haven Hotel.

"If you hear anything about Kimball—or happen to spot him—get in touch with me. I'll make it worth your while."

"You mean—" Cushman patted his vest pocket, causing the two gold coins it contained to clink together.

"I hope I'll hear from you," Sutton told him and left the building.

As he walked the familiar streets on his way to Dupont Street, he found himself fondly remembering his last visit to San Francisco. The city was, he mused, as brawny as a longshoreman and as beautiful as a pampered courtesan. It had been sired by the forty-niners and was growing up to be an odd mixture of wealth and culture, sinfulness and danger. A city which made a man feel not only vibrantly alive but overjoyed to be so while he remained aware that the seamy side of this city by the sea could not only tempt but threaten.

Lost in his thoughts, he passed the building that was his destination. Recovering himself, he retraced his steps and stopped for a moment in front of the three-story clapboard structure that bore a discreet sign above its entrance which read Magdalen House. He climbed the steps and used the brass knocker on the door.

The door was opened a moment later by a woman who was busily engaged in pinning in place escaped strands of her hair while she was as busily engaged in calling out instructions to a number of Oriental girls who were clustered behind her in the hallway.

She's an attractive woman, Sutton thought, as he noted her oval face, creamy complexion, soft hair, and softer brown eyes. She wore a yellow cotton day dress with a boned bodice, stand collar, and fitted sleeves. It was trimmed at the wrists and skirt with amber braid.

"Good day to you, sir," she greeted Sutton, and then called out, "Girls, stop fussing and please *try*, do, to be little ladies!"

Her admonition had little effect on her charges, who

simpered, whimpered, giggled, cast shy or sly glances in Sutton's direction, and continued to fidget constantly.

One of the girls, whom Sutton judged to be no more than sixteen, turned and spoke harshly but briefly to the others in Chinese. They immediately quieted. They lowered their eyes. They stood still as stones.

The woman in the doorway sighed with relief. Talking more to herself than to Sutton, she said, "I just do not know how I shall ever manage when Ah Toy is gone. She has a way with the other girls that is almost magical. A word from Ah Toy and the others become altogether *angelic.*" Then, as if suddenly becoming aware once again of Sutton's presence on her doorstep, she blushed and said, "I am so sorry, sir. Is there something you wish?"

"I'm here to pay a call on Miss Roberta Pritchard."

"I am at your service, sir."

"Miss Pritchard, my name's Luke Sutton. I was given your name by the janitor of the building in which Mr. Theodore Kimball has his office. I—"

"Is he hurt? Ted, I mean? Oh, I just knew something awful had happened to him."

"Hold on, Miss Pritchard. I came here because I was told you were a client of Kimball's and I hoped you'd be able to tell me where I might find him."

"Me? Oh, dear me, no. I have no idea where Ted is. I haven't seen him since he left for Virginia City, and that was some time ago. I've been terribly worried about him. Are you a friend of his, Mr. Sutton?"

Sutton dodged the question by asking one of his own. "Where does Kimball live, Miss Pritchard?"

She gave him Kimball's address. "But he's not at home. I've gone there—and to his office—every day, including today, since the day Ted was due back from Virginia City, and no one has seen him at either location. Ted has

not been to his home or his office. His landlady agrees
with me. We both think he may have met with foul play.
It is not at all like Ted to simply vanish of his own free
will from the face of the earth, which he does seem to
have done."

She doesn't know, Sutton thought, that her attorney-
at-law's wanted for murder.

"Mr. Sutton, I really must excuse myself. I have to
escort these girls to the waterfront, where a boat awaits
them. We are late as it is, and we dare not miss that boat,
which is to return the girls to China. Good day to you,
sir."

"If you've not got any objections, Miss Pritchard, I'll
walk along with you. It's a nice day for a stroll and I
could use the exercise."

"As you like, Mr. Sutton. Girls— Ah Toy, we're ready
to go now. Just let me get my bonnet."

As Miss Pritchard disappeared into a room opening off
the hall, the girl named Ah Toy gave Sutton a smile that
had in it, he thought, all the guilelessness of childhood
and all the wily worldliness of an experienced woman.
He touched the brim of his hat to her and then Miss
Pritchard was back, tying under her chin the ribbons of
the gathered fawn bonnet she was wearing.

Sutton stood to one side, and, led by Ah Toy, the girls
left the building and began to troop demurely down Dupont Street. He followed Miss Pritchard down the steps
and then walked in silence beside her as they both followed Ah Toy and the other girls.

Miss Pritchard broke the silence by asking, "Do you
think something unfortunate has happened to Ted—to
Mr. Kimball, Mr. Sutton?"

It's time, he thought, for me to toss my cards on the
table and stop pussyfooting around. "Miss Pritchard,

something unfortunate sure has happened to Kimball. He's become a murderer."

She gasped and stopped in her tracks.

Sutton turned to face her.

"I don't believe you. What you just said—it's incredible. Ted a murderer?" She tried a laugh, which emerged from her mouth as another gasp.

"It's true, Miss Pritchard," Sutton assured her, and then he proceeded to tell her about the murder of Dade McGrath and how he was hunting Kimball for the bounty money, ending his account with, "So Kimball killed Dade McGrath on account of he thought the man was paying impolite attention to Miss Fern Thorndyke. And like I just said, Miss Thorndyke at first tried lying to cover up for Kimball but ended up telling the truth about the murder to the sheriff, who also got Marcus Proctor, the man I just mentioned to you, to admit that Kimball had confessed to him that he'd brained McGrath with a poker when he saw what McGrath was trying to do to Miss Thorndyke."

Miss Pritchard, obviously dazed by what she had just heard, suddenly sprang to life and hurried after her charges, leaving Sutton behind her.

He caught up with her, and when he was once again walking by her side, he commented, "The fact that your friend Kimball's gone to ground doesn't make him out to be the most innocent of men."

"Ted is no murderer!"

"If he's not, he ought to turn himself in to the authorities in Virginia City and defend himself against the charge they've got leveled against him back there. And anybody who knows anything about his present whereabouts—well, Miss Pritchard, I'm not a lawyer, but it seems to me that anybody who tries to cover up for Kimball could be in for some legal trouble of their own."

"Are you threatening me, Mr. Sutton?"

"Nope, I'm not. I'm just trying every way I know how to tell you I need your help."

"My help?"

"Should you hear from him or see Kimball—let me know. I'm staying at the Sailors' Haven Hotel."

"Turn Ted in to a—a bounty hunter?"

Sutton heard the contempt with which Miss Pritchard had uttered her last two words. She looked at him as if she were about to spit in his face.

"I may be a bounty hunter, Miss Pritchard, but I'm not a judge nor am I a jury."

She opened her mouth to speak, her eyes angry, when a scream from one of the girls walking in front of her and Sutton silenced her. She halted. And then, when she saw the stocky pigtailed Chinese plow his way into the midst of her charges, she gasped, her hand reaching out to seize Sutton's arm, an expression that combined alarm and amazement on her face.

Sutton shook himself free of her and went charging into the midst of the girls. They scattered before him like frightened chickens. In the distance ahead of him Ah Toy took flight. Behind her sped the Chinese, his hands reaching out to seize her. Sutton pursued them both, gradually narrowing the distance between himself and his quarry, unmindful as he raced on of the startled looks that passersby were giving him or of the shrill cries of Miss Pritchard's girls behind him.

He reached out and grabbed the shoulder of the Chinese who was pursuing Ah Toy. He spun him around and slammed his right fist into the man's startled face. Then, releasing him, he delivered a swift series of punishing body blows that left the Chinese bent over, clutching his stomach, and gagging.

But a moment later, the man straightened and lunged at Sutton, his long-nailed fingers reaching for Sutton's throat. Sutton stepped back and slapped the man's hands away. He drew back his left arm and then let loose a haymaker that crashed into the jaw of the Chinese, snapping the man's head backward and sending his pigtail flying through the air.

Sutton stood his ground, his fists ready. "Get out of here," he muttered.

The Chinese backed up, his dark eyes gleaming as they searched Sutton's face as if making an effort to memorize its every feature. Then, speaking in Chinese, the man straightened and pointed a stiff finger in Sutton's direction. A moment later he turned and raced away.

"Oh, thank you, Mr. Sutton!"

Sutton turned to find Miss Pritchard hurrying toward him, her girls hurrying along in a tight group right behind her.

"What was that all about, do you now?" he asked her.

"That man was Ming Long. He is the head of the Kwong Dock tong here in San Francisco. He is an importer of Chinese girls like those I try to rescue. He arranges to buy them from their impoverished parents and also, in far too many cases, to kidnap young girls, all of whom, once they arrive here in America, are forced into prostitution—into a life of sexual slavery. Perhaps you have heard of the cribs and parlor houses in Chinatown."

Sutton nodded, thinking of the sumptuously furnished and heavily incensed houses on Grant Avenue and Waverly Place that were the occasional targets of the police and the press and of the dingy cribs like those he had seen that lined both sides of notorious China Alley which extended from Jackson Street to Washington Street.

"I have been fighting men like Ming Long for more years than I care to remember," Miss Pritchard remarked somewhat wistfully. "I have won, I must confess to you, very few of our battles." She looked up at Sutton, and he saw determination in the thrust of her chin and the light blazing in her eyes. "But I will not give up the fight. If I am able to save one child from a life of utter degradation —" As if remembering something, she spun around to where her girls stood clustered together behind her. "Ah Toy?" She spoke in Chinese to the girls who shook their heads.

She turned back to Sutton. "Ah Toy is gone! Ming Long must have taken her!"

"He didn't," Sutton stated flatly. "She ran off after I got my hands on Ming Long."

"I must find her before Ming Long or any of his tong members do. You see, Mr. Sutton, Ming Long bought Ah Toy in China and sold her to a wealthy white man here in town. But then Ted Kimball brought Ah Toy to me when he happened to discover her hiding in the streets one night after she had escaped from the man who bought her. At that time, Ted had just begun to represent me and Magdalen House in the courts. I warned him that he had made a bitter enemy in the person of Ming Long, but he only laughed. I must warn you too, Mr. Sutton. I heard what Ming Long said to you.

"I can speak a little—very little, I'm afraid—Chinese, but I can understand much more when I hear it spoken. Ming Long vowed to destroy you to salvage his honor which you, by beating him so badly, have besmirched. Now you, Mr. Sutton, are as much of an enemy in Ming Long's eyes as is Ted for having helped Ah Toy escape from him and the man to whom he sold her. Ming Long must kill you now if his honor is to be restored to him."

"Well, I whipped him once. I reckon I can whip him again if he shows up to pester me anytime in the future."

"You don't understand. Not only will Ming Long try to kill you now, but so will each of the members of the Kwong Dock tong. By insulting Ming Long, you have also insulted the tong. Surely you can see that you are in great danger now?"

"It's not the first time I've been in it, nor is it likely to be the last, given the kind of life I do seem bound and determined to lead." Sutton grinned. "Miss Pritchard, you take your girls to their boat. I'll go look for Ah Toy. I'll meet you back at the mission and let you know if I had any luck."

"Thank you ever so much, Mr. Sutton—"

"Luke."

"Be careful—Luke."

He touched the brim of his hat to her and then turned and sprinted down the street in the direction Ah Toy had taken.

FIVE

That night Sutton returned to Magdalen House and was admitted to the building by Roberta Pritchard.

"Did you find Ah Toy?" she asked anxiously.

He shook his head.

"I thought not. If you had found her, you would have brought her back here with you."

"That girl's disappeared like a whisper in a big wind," Sutton remarked. "But I'll keep my eyes open, and should I chance to see her, I'll tell her you're real worried about her, Miss Pritchard."

"Please call me Roberta, Luke. May I ask what you plan to do now?"

"You mean about Kimball?"

"Yes."

"I'm going to keep on hunting him, though I'm not sure where to start to tell you the plain truth. San Francisco's a big place." Sutton paused, his eyes on Roberta. The idea that had just struck him, he thought, might work. It was, he decided, worth a try. "I just hope I find Kimball before Ming Long does."

Roberta's body stiffened. She stared at Sutton, uneasiness in her eyes.

"I at least intend to take Kimball alive if I can, but that Ming Long— From what you told me about him earlier today, I reckon he'll kill Kimball if he can find him."

"I was thinking this afternoon," Roberta murmured.

"You were? About what?" Sutton was sure his reference to Ming Long and the man's intentions in regard to Kimball had done the trick. She's coming over to my side, he thought. At least I hope she is.

"I was leaving Ted's law office one day," Roberta said. "There was a man in the waiting room—a most disreputable-looking man. Ted later told me that he was one of the denizens of the Barbary Coast who had gotten into trouble with the law, and Ted, for a most modest fee, had agreed to represent the man whom he described to me as 'friendless and forlorn.' I remembered the man this afternoon and I thought I should mention him to you. His name is Buzzer Dunn. Ted said he was an employee of a woman he called Lady Dora, who, I gather, owns a disreputable establishment—a dive, to be blunt about it—on the Barbary Coast, known as the Cowboy's Rest.

"I thought I should mention Mr. Dunn to you, Luke, in case you should want to talk to him about Ted. Perhaps Mr. Dunn knows where Ted is. I've wracked my brain and can't come up with any other names of people whom Ted has had contact with in either his personal or professional life. There is, of course, his landlady, as I mentioned to you at our first meeting, but—"

"I stopped by to see her on my way here. She couldn't —or wouldn't—give me any information. I asked her if Kimball was close to any of her other boarders, and she told me she's got a whole new crew of them since Kimball left for Virginia City and she doesn't know where any of the men who boarded with her when Kimball was there are to be found now."

"Do you think Mr. Dunn might be of some help to you, Luke?"

"Can't say for certain. But I'm obliged to you for mentioning him to me. I'll go see if I can find him. And if I do

—well, I've not got another lead to Kimball, so my best bet at the moment, seems like, is to talk to Buzzer Dunn. I'm obliged to you, Miss—Roberta."

"Be careful, Luke. It seems I'm always saying that to you. But the Barbary Coast is a decidedly unsavory part of the city and is infested with thugs and hoodlums."

"I'll keep in touch, Roberta. And I'd be obliged to you, like I said before, if you'd get in touch with me at the Sailors' Haven Hotel if you come up with anything about Kimball that you think I ought to know."

Roberta started to speak but then frowned instead.

"Something fretting you?"

"To be quite frank about it, Luke, yes, there is something bothering me. I'm really not sure that I can trust you. If I should hear from Ted—or learn his whereabouts —how do I know you won't kill him?"

"I guess you don't know, Roberta. But I can tell you this. I'm not a bloodthirsty man. All I'm doing is looking to take Kimball back to Virginia City to stand trial. I'm not out to kill him. But Ming Long—speaking of bloodthirsty, like I just was—now he strikes me as a man who could wear that label, and judging by what you told me, he's hunting Kimball same as me."

Roberta sighed. "I shall get in touch with you at once if I learn anything about Ted that might help you find him."

Sutton nodded his thanks and then left Magdalen House.

Following the directions he had received from a passerby he had questioned, Sutton walked down the Barbary Coast's Davis Street, and when he came to the Cowboy's Rest, he entered the saloon.

The smoke that filled the air inside the low-ceilinged

dive almost choked him. He coughed and fought the impulse to turn around and leave the place that resounded with a fearsome blend of noise made by a nickelodeon, the shouts of men, the screeching of women, and the thudding of dancers' feet that were hitting the floor's bare boards.

Sutton, his resolve stiffening, shouldered his way through the crowd that was more a drunken mob. On his way to the bar, a bleary-eyed woman wearing a low-cut red velvet gown appeared like a weary apparition out of the smoke and put her arms around him.

"Buy a girl a drink, cowboy?"

Sutton slapped away the woman's hands that were clumsily easing into the pocket of his jeans in search of his money. He set her aside, ignored the obscene name she called him, and plowed on through the thick crowd. When he reached the bar, a gaudily painted crone behind it asked him what he'd have.

"Whiskey," he answered, and a bottle and glass were promptly plopped down in front of him on the bar's wet surface.

Sutton filled his glass. He raised it to the woman behind the bar. "Long life." He was about to take a drink when the woman seized his wrist, almost spilling his whiskey.

"You trying to act smart with Lady Dora, are you?"

"I don't know what you mean."

" 'Long life' indeed!" she snapped. "I may not be young anymore, but there's a whole lot of life left in this old lady, and I won't take insults from fresh-faced dudes who've got no respect for their elders."

"Beg pardon, ma'am," Sutton said, regretting his gaffe. "To your good health."

Lady Dora released her hold on him. She smiled. He

drank. She leaned over the bar toward him and whispered in his ear. He grinned and told her he'd picked up a disease from one of the working girls over in China Alley, so he had to decline her blunt invitation, not wanting to infect his newfound friend.

"Actually," he continued, lowering his voice to a conspiratorial whisper and then having to raise it because the noise in the room kept him from being heard, "I'm not here on pleasure so much as I'm here on business. I'm looking for a man named Buzzer Dunn."

Lady Dora abruptly drew back from Sutton. "You don't look like a cop."

"I assure you I'm not one, Lady Dora," he said quickly, thinking that her reaction certainly told him a lot about the man named Buzzer Dunn. "I've got a job that needs doing and I was told that Mr. Dunn is the slick sort of man that can do it for me. The job I have in mind's worth fifty dollars to Dunn—if he's interested in doing it."

Lady Dora pointed out a man lounging at the far end of the bar. "That's Buzzer. The one with the split upper lip and stocking cap on."

"I'm obliged to you." Sutton placed a dollar on the bar, touched the brim of his hat to Lady Dora, and then made his way down the bar.

When he reached Buzzer Dunn, he stepped up beside the man and said, "You and me, Dunn, we have a mutual acquaintance."

Dunn glared at him.

Sutton glared back, noting Dunn's bushy black mustache that was stained with either blood or ketchup, his sallow complexion, his pockmarked cheeks, his pale blue eyes.

"Shove off, mate," Dunn muttered and picked up his bottle of beer.

He was about to put it to his mouth when Sutton seized his arm, pulling it down, and said, "Ted Kimball's the name of the man we both know."

Dunn shook his arm free of Sutton's grip. "So what?"

"Kimball's dropped out of sight. I want to find him. I was told you might be able to help me do that."

"By who?"

"Never mind about that. Do you know where Kimball's been keeping himself lately?" Sutton's hand slipped into and then out of his pocket. His eyes on Dunn, he flipped the eagle in his hand.

Dunn caught and pocketed it. "You've come to the right man," he told Sutton. He took Sutton's arm and, abandoning his bottle of beer, led him down the bar to a spot where no one stood, although the rest of the room was densely packed with people. "We can talk more private here," Dunn said, beckoning to Lady Dora. When she stood across the bar from him, he ordered beer. "What'll you have, mister?" he asked Sutton.

"Whiskey."

Dunn beckoned to Lady Dora. "Give my friend here a good stiff shot of your special blend."

When their drinks had been served, Dunn clinked his bottle against Sutton's glass. "What's Kimball to you?"

"Do you know where he is?" Sutton asked, ignoring Dunn's question and sipping his whiskey, which he found to be stronger than any he had ever tasted before and slightly bitter.

"I know where he is. But that kind of knowledge comes dear. It's not the kind of knowledge a man can buy for a measly ten dollars."

Sutton, suppressing a sense of elation, began to won-

der if Dunn was telling him the truth. There was, he
realized, simply no way of knowing. Maybe Dunn was
just leading him on, trying to take him for whatever
money he could. He suspected that such might very well
be the case. On the other hand, he reasoned, I can't just
walk away from Dunn, write him off. Maybe he does
know where Kimball is.

"Drink up," Dunn muttered, pointing to Sutton's
glass.

Sutton drank. Grimaced.

"Lady Dora's special blend'll put hair on your chest
and fire in your eyes," Dunn remarked with a grin that
was first cousin to a sneer.

The whiskey burned its way down into Sutton's stomach, and for a split second, he thought he was about to
retch. His eyes began to water. The smoke, he thought.
He started to sweat. It's hot in here, he told himself.
Buzzer Dunn began to sway before his eyes. Sutton put
out a hand to try to steady the man—and missed Dunn
entirely. He suddenly staggered. He reached out for the
bar to keep himself from falling. As he did so, the room
began to whirl around him. And then he knew. *The whiskey.* What Dunn had called Lady Dora's special blend. It
was drugged, he thought, as points of red light danced in
front of his eyes, beyond which he could just make out
the figures of Lady Dora and Buzzer Dunn, who were
both leering at him. Drugged with something, he
thought. I've got to—

He never completed the thought, because at that instant the floor fell out from under him and he went hur-
tling downward, limbs akimbo, his hat falling off. Seconds later, he struck a pile of sour-smelling mattresses on
the floor of a room beneath the saloon, which broke his

fall. As he did so, he felt himself sinking down into a deep and overwhelming darkness.

A stench invaded Sutton's nostrils. His stomach heaved as a result of its overpowering onslaught. Opening his eyes was an effort, but he finally succeeded in doing so, only to confront a blackness that was almost as deep as the one from which he had just emerged. Stars, he thought as he gazed up at the night sky that was blurry above him and reached for his gun. Gone, he thought with a blend of anger and dismay as his hand struck his empty holster. He heaved himself up on his elbows, the sharp pain in his head briefly blinding him as he did so, and looked around to discover that he was in a skiff which he recognized as a Whitehall boat. His spirits sank. I've been shanghaied, he thought. He discovered that he was surrounded on all sides by the limp bodies of men, none of whom seemed to be conscious. He turned his head and caught a starlit glimpse of the oarsman. Beside him sat another man, equally as grim-faced, with Sutton's cocked revolver in his right hand.

"So you're awake, are you, mate?" the armed man said to Sutton, and then spat a stream of tobacco juice over the side of the skiff. "And by now you've probably figured out what's happened to you. And as if that weren't clever enough of you, now you're thinking that you'd best jump overboard and start swimming for shore else you'll not see San Francisco again for more years than you can maybe count. Well, me bucko, you take a dive and you're dead. I'll fill you so full of lead out of this here Colt of yours that you'll sink in less than a minute."

Sutton suppressed a groan.

"You never should have gotten mixed up with Buzzer Dunn and Lady Dora, mate," volunteered the oarsman in a cheerful tone. "They're poison, that pair is. I've got a whole crew here for the *Mary Malone*, I have, thanks to Lady Dora and Buzzer—and thanks too to Lady Dora's special blend of laudanum-laced whiskey and the trapdoor she's got in her barroom floor."

"The *Mary Malone*—where's she bound out for?" Sutton muttered through clenched teeth.

"The Philippines, South America, Cuba—"

"We're here!" snarled the armed man as they drew alongside a ship that bore the painted name *Mary Malone* and which loomed above the skiff like a leviathan beside a sardine.

The oarsman secured the skiff to the ship with a line, stood up, and proceeded to kick the men littering the bottom of the skiff into consciousness.

Groaning and muttering gruff but ineffective protests, all but two of the men got groggily to their feet. Then, under the verbal goading and physical prodding of the oarsman and the shouted threats of his armed companion, they began to climb the ladder to the main deck of the *Mary Malone*.

"Up you go, laddie," barked the oarsman, and Sutton climbed the Jacob's ladder that was hanging over the side of the ship. He emerged on deck to find some of the shanghaied men sprawled on the deck while others stood swaying by the rail.

Moments later the oarsman arrived on deck, a body slung over his shoulder. He dropped it to the deck and then climbed back down the ladder. He returned with another body draped over his shoulder, which he also dropped unceremoniously on the deck.

He broke into a broad smile as a man emerged from the forecastle and grimaced when he saw the men standing and lying on the deck.

"Evening to you, captain!" the oarsman called out to him. "Isn't it a lovely night now?"

"Do you dare to call that load of wharf rats able-bodied seamen?" roared the captain. "They're weaklings, all but that one"—he pointed to Sutton—"and even he'll not last the full three years till we berth here again."

Three years! The words echoed dismally in Sutton's mind.

"Ah, is it dissatisfied you are, captain? Now sorry it is I am to hear that. Then there's nothing for it but to dispose of all this merchandise you find so unsatisfactory."

"Unsatisfactory?" echoed the captain. "*Unacceptable!*" he bellowed.

The oarsman nodded to his armed companion, who fired a shot that shattered the skull of a man standing beside Sutton. As the man went down in a bloody heap, the oarsman, addressing his companion, gloated, "Good shooting! Now if you'll be so kind as to dispose of the rest of this unsatisfactory—nay, *unacceptable*—merchandise—"

"*No!*" shouted the captain. "Stay your hand, sir."

Self-satisfied smiles wreathed the faces of the oarsman and his burly companion who had just committed murder.

The captain cursed under his breath and then began to pace the deck, his hands clasped behind his back, his eyes darting among the men who had been shanghaied to serve as his crew. "You've got me over a barrel and you damn well know it," he muttered, addressing the oarsman and the man in possession of Sutton's revolver. "I need crewmen—"

"And now you've gone and gotten yourself some fine ones, captain, sir," mocked the oarsman, his evil little eyes glinting in the starlight.

"But not enough. I'm still short of men and—"

"We'll get you more, captain," said the oarsman soothingly, "so rest easy on that score."

"—and these at fifty dollars a head—why, they're not worth ten. *Five!*" The captain erupted in another rowdy string of curses. He kicked one of the two bodies the oarsman had earlier dumped on the deck.

"The time's come to settle your account with us," declared the oarsman as he hurriedly approached the captain and held out his hand.

But the captain ignored him. He bent down and shook the man he had just kicked. He shook him a second time, and Sutton saw the man's head loll to the left at an impossible angle.

"What's this?" snapped the captain, bending even closer to examine the man lying on the deck. "What have we here, my mates?" And then the captain straightened and seized the oarsman by the lapels of his jacket and shook him the way a cat shakes a rat it is trying to kill. "That man is dead!" the captain shouted. "His neck's been broken."

"He was quick when we put him aboard our Whitehall boat," the oarsman bellowed, struggling to free himself from the captain's grasp and failing to do so. "I swear he was!"

"Liar!" the captain roared and shook the oarsman again. Then, suddenly releasing the man, he kicked the other body lying on the deck beside the dead man.

Sutton heard a series of shrill squeals that followed the kick. He watched the body quiver.

"Get up!" ordered the captain at the top of his voice. When his order wasn't immediately obeyed, he bent down and hauled the body to its feet.

"We want our money," the oarsman said nervously.

"And we want it now," the man beside him added ominously, brandishing Sutton's gun at the captain, who gave them both a contemptuous glance and then, after drawing a knife from his belt, used it to slice through the clothes of the body he was holding upright.

Sutton was startled to see two huge rats leap through the rent the captain had made in the clothes and go scampering across the deck to vanish in the darkness.

"Old clothes!" the captain cried, shaking what had appeared to be a body in both of his hands. "Old clothes you stuffed and in which you imprisoned rats to make them move in order to deceive me into believing this stuffed dummy was a man's body. Get off my ship, you brazen scoundrels!"

"We'll get," said the oarsman with surprising equanimity. "But we'll take your crew with us, captain, sir."

"Let's go, boys," the gunman called out as if on cue. "Over the side, boys, and back into the skiff."

As the shanghaied men scurried eagerly toward the Jacob's ladder that was hanging over the side of the ship, the captain stepped in front of them to block their progress. "I'll pay you for the live ones," he told the oarsman with obvious reluctance. "But not for the dead man, the dummy, nor the man you murdered. But I'll do so only because I am a desperate man and you have taken unseemly advantage of my plight."

The oarsman thrust out a dirty hand. The armed man ordered the crewmen-to-be to stand back, and then he turned his attention to the money the captain was counting and reluctantly placing in the oarsman's eagerly outstretched hand.

Sutton elbowed his way into the midst of the shanghaied men. "We outnumber those three," he whispered. "We can take them!"

"That murdering son of a bitch has a gun," one of the men pointed out nervously.

"It's mine, and I intend to take it back from him while you boys go after the other one and the captain."

"We could be killed!" protested one of the men in the crowd in a whiskey-coarsened voice.

"We could be," Sutton agreed. "But it's either take your chances with me or set sail on that three-year-long voyage the captain's planning. Which is it going to be, boys?"

Their answer was a simultaneous move made by all of them in the direction of their buyer and seller.

Sutton eased out of the crowd and moved as noiselessly and as unnoticeably as a shadow toward the man armed with his .45. He stepped to one side in order to remain out of the man's line of vision, and as he did so, he cast a glance over his shoulder. He halted, waiting for the other men who had been shanghaied to make their move. Then as they all surged forward toward the retreating oarsman and the captain, Sutton sprang forward, seized the man who had his gun, and threw him down on the deck. He wrested his gun from the startled man's hand as angry shouts erupted behind him. Placing one booted foot on the decked man's chest and aiming the gun at his gut, Sutton glanced over his shoulder and saw a pile of bodies rolling about on the deck. Arms and legs sprouted from the roiling mass of flesh which looked like some bizarre and never before seen organism and which was shouting with countless voices, some shrill, some hoarse, some gleeful. He turned his attention back to the man he had downed.

"It's clear to me," he said stonily, "that you and your partner are in cahoots with Lady Dora and Buzzer Dunn. She served me that doctored whiskey, and he set me up so I was standing right on top of that trapdoor that dropped me down into that basement room. That's when you boys took over. Now what I want to know from you is where I can find Buzzer Dunn. I've got a score to settle with that man who ought to call himself Buzzard, not Buzzer."

"You want money?" the man cried out as he stared fearfully up at Sutton and at the leveled .45 in Sutton's hard hand. "We'll give you money. Only don't shoot—"

"I just told you what I wanted." Sutton rammed his boot heel into the man's chest.

The man on the deck groaned and grabbed Sutton's boot with both hands but he couldn't dislodge it.

"Talk!"

"Buzzer holes up in a boardinghouse over Shanghai Kelly's Saloon. It's on Pacific Street between Drumm and Davis streets. Number 33."

A roar went up from behind Sutton. He turned and saw the oarsman being held high and horizontally in the air by the hands of several men. The oarsman continued roaring, the wordless sound both a protest against the way he was being treated and a plea that he be released.

Sutton let out a roar of his own as the man he had decked suddenly seized his boot and twisted his ankle. He knew he was going down despite his frantic efforts to maintain his balance. And he did. As he hit the deck, the companion of the oarsman leaped to his feet and went racing away toward the railing.

Sutton quickly scrambled to his feet, his finger tightening reflexively on the trigger of his Colt. But he didn't fire. Instead, he leathered the gun and went after the man who had gotten away from him. He caught up with him at the railing, and before the man could jump overboard, he seized him by the shoulder, spun him around, and gave him a hard right uppercut that snapped the man's head backward and bent his body over the railing.

Sutton reached out and grabbed the man's coat, pulling him away from the railing before he could fall overboard. This time he hurled a left jab, a right cross, and then a short-arced punch to the gut. He stepped back, expecting the man to go down. But the man did not go down. He threw his head up, fisted both of his hands, and came snarling at Sutton like a flesh-and-bone battering ram.

Sutton took a harmless blow on his left shoulder and then another far from harmless one that smashed against the left side of his face. He retaliated with a pair of hard-flung haymakers, and then as his attacker tried to knee him in the groin, he kicked out with his right foot, and the heel of his boot slammed into the man's rising kneecap. He heard with grim satisfaction the snap of bone, and he listened with no sympathy to the anguished cry of the man who seized his kneecap and began to hobble screaming about the deck.

Sutton heard a loud splash, but he didn't turn to see what had caused it, unwilling to make the mistake he had made earlier by turning his attention away from the man he had had pinned to the deck.

Another splash.

And then the mob of shanghaied men came careening into Sutton's line of vision. They descended on the oarsman's companion, who was still howling and still clutching the kneecap Sutton had broken, and as unmindful of the man's agonized cries as was Sutton himself, they lifted him up bodily until he was being held in a horizontal position above their heads, carried him to the rail, and threw him overboard.

Sutton knew now what had caused the two earlier

splashes he had heard. The bodies of the captain and the oarsman, he thought. He made his way to where the Jacob's ladder hung over the side of the ship and began to climb down it. Once he was in the Whitehall boat again, he seated himself, freed the line that held the skiff to the *Mary Malone,* and began to row away from the ship.

A man appeared at the railing above him, waving a bottle. "We've found the captain's store of rum," the man shouted down to Sutton. "Come on back up here, mate, and join the party!"

The man was joined by others. Bottles of rum were waved in the air and then tilted against lips.

Sutton gave the men a wave and continued rowing away from the *Mary Malone.*

"Bon voyage!" one of the men yelled to him from the deck, and then they all disappeared from the railing, only the sound of their bibulous laughter and raucous shouting testifying to their presence on the ship.

Sutton rowed on and then suddenly found himself unable to move the oar in his right hand. He pulled at it. It remained motionless. And then a head broke the surface of the water followed by two hands which were gripping the other end of the oar.

The man who had earlier taken Sutton's gun jerked the oar out of Sutton's hand and, brandishing it, began to climb aboard the skiff. When he was halfway into the boat, he swung the oar, striking Sutton and knocking him backward.

Recovering quickly, Sutton jerked the other oar out of its lock, and as the dripping man climbed all the way into the boat, the oar raised high above his head and about to descend, Sutton swung the oar in his hands and it cracked against his attacker's ribs, knocking the man overboard.

Sutton got to his knees and reached out to retrieve the oar the man had dropped, which was floating on the surface of the starlit water.

He spotted a man climbing the *Mary Malone*'s Jacob's ladder. As he watched the man climbing up toward the deck of the ship, he saw a second man emerge from the water and begin to climb the ladder. From his distant position on the bay, he couldn't identify either of the men. He rowed rapidly on, heading for shore, his eyes fixed on the Jacob's ladder as a third man broke the surface of the bay and began to climb it.

SIX

As he entered the lobby of the Sailors' Haven Hotel, Sutton was wearing the crisp new Stetson he had just bought to replace the hat he had lost in Lady Dora's Cowboy's Rest.

He was starting up the steps to the second floor when the desk clerk called his name and beckoned to him. He retraced his steps, and when he reached the desk, the clerk leaned over it and, pointing to a Chinese woman seated demurely on the far side of the lobby, whispered, "She's been here all day, Mr. Sutton. She asked for you, and when I gave her your room number, she went there and then returned and said you were not in and that she would wait for you if I didn't mind."

"I'm obliged to you." Sutton crossed the lobby and stopped in front of the woman who, looking up at him hopefully, asked, "Are you by any chance Mr. Luke Sutton?"

"I am," Sutton answered, admiring her smooth complexion, straight black hair, almond eyes, and pale lips. "And you're—"

"My name is Loi Yan. May we go to your room, Mr. Sutton? I have something important I want very much to discuss with you."

"Sure we can."

The woman rose, took Sutton's arm, and he escorted her across the lobby and up the stairs. Once inside his room, he waited until she had seated herself in the only chair in the room, and then, leaning against the window's sill, his arms folded across his chest, he asked, "What's on your mind, Loi Yan?"

"A good friend of mine. Her name is Ah Toy. You remember the name, Mr. Sutton?"

"I do."

"I work for Miss Roberta Pritchard at Magdalen House, Mr. Sutton. I learned earlier today from her that Ming Long of the Kwong Dock tong tried to abduct Ah Toy while she was with you and Miss Pritchard and the other girls and that Ah Toy fled and has not been seen since."

Loi Yan continued in her well-modulated voice, "Miss Pritchard also mentioned to me that you told her that Mr. Theodore Kimball, who befriended Ah Toy, is wanted for murder in Virginia City and that you are here in San Francisco in the hope of finding Mr. Kimball —so that you may collect the bounty being offered for him."

"All that's the truth," Sutton admitted. "Now what I'm wondering is how come you're here, Loi Yan. I mean, what is it you figure I can do for you?"

"You can stop hunting Mr. Kimball."

"I can stop—" Sutton chuckled, shook his head. "No, ma'am, I can't do that."

"You mean you won't."

"You could put it that way."

Loi Yan's eyes caught fire briefly, but the fire in them quickly died. "Ah Toy told me one day not so long ago that when Mr. Kimball first found and befriended her— that was before he brought her to Miss Pritchard at Magdalen House—he had offered her the use of a refuge where, he assured her, she would be quite safe. Now it is my theory that Ah Toy may very well be at this moment once again in that refuge. When she fled from Ming Long, she may have returned to it. Where else could she go?"

"She might have. Where is this place of Kimball's?"

"I don't know where it is. Ah Toy never told me and at the time I had no interest in knowing its whereabouts."

"But now you do want to know where this hideout is that you think Ah Toy might be at."

"That is correct. And as far as I know, based on what Ah Toy told me, only two people know the location of that refuge. Ah Toy herself, of course—"

"And Ted Kimball."

"Yes. And you"—Loi Yan rose and crossed the room to stand directly in front of Sutton—"have threatened to kill Mr. Kimball."

"Nope. I never did do that. I told Miss Pritchard that I—"

"If you were to kill Mr. Kimball, Mr. Sutton"—Loi Yan turned away from him—"I might never be able to find Ah Toy. She will be afraid to show herself on the streets. She will be afraid to return to the mission, where Ming Long might come after her."

Loi Yan turned back to Sutton, her arms folded in front of her, her hands tucked into the full sleeves of the tight silk sheath she was wearing. "I intend to do my very best to locate Mr. Kimball," she declared stoutly, "in the hope that he can tell me where to find Ah Toy. I will not let you kill him, Mr. Sutton."

Sutton was about to protest again that he hoped he would not have to kill—or even wound—Kimball if he succeeded in finding him, but before he could utter a word, Loi Yan's hands were suddenly withdrawn from the sleeves of her dress. He twisted his body just in time as she attempted to stab him with the dagger in her right hand. It struck the butt of his .45 instead of plunging deep into his body.

He seized her wrist and twisted it, causing her to cry out in pain, bend backward, and a moment later drop the dagger.

"Damn you!" he shouted at her. "I ought to—"

He never got to finish whatever it was he had been about to say, because Loi Yan chose that moment to bend over and bite his wrist. She tore savagely at it with her teeth, drawing blood.

As he yelped and released her, she turned and fled from the room. By the time he reached the hall, she had already disappeared. He sprinted to the top of the stairs and caught a glimpse of her just before she ran from the hotel's lobby and disappeared in the crowd of people passing by outside.

The following morning Sutton arrived at Magdalen House and pounded loudly on its door, which was promptly opened by Roberta Pritchard.

"Why, Luke," she exclaimed. "I wasn't expecting you. But it's good to see you again. Do come in, please."

When they were seated in the mission's parlor, Sutton said, "A woman you've got working here tried to kill me last night."

Roberta's eyes widened. A hand flew up to flutter against her breast. "A woman—who?"

"Her name, she told me, is Loi Yan."

"Loi Yan," Roberta repeated. "But—but why, Luke? I mean, I don't understand."

"You told Loi Yan about me. Me and Kimball."

"Why, yes, I did. We spoke after your first visit."

"Well, to answer your question, it seems Loi Yan and Ah Toy are real good friends."

"Yes, that's true. Actually, they are more like sisters. Closer than mere friends ordinarily are. But what has Ah Toy to do with Loi Yan's attempt on your life?"

Sutton told Roberta what Loi Yan had told him, concluding with, "Then she tried to stab me with a dagger she had hidden on her somewhere."

"Oh, the poor misguided girl!" Roberta exclaimed.

"She's not so much misguided, Roberta, as she is murderous." Sutton paused and then said, "This hunt of mine for Kimball, it's turning out to be downright dangerous. It appears there are a whole bunch of treacherous people out to do me in to keep me, for one reason or another, from getting to Kimball. There was a hardcase back in Virginia City—a man name of Bad Ed Kelvin—who tried to gun me down. I don't know who hired him, but somebody did, that's for certain. Then on the trail west I ran into the brother of the man Kimball killed, and he—his name's Lorne McGrath—tried to do me in. At a stage stop along the way two friends of Kimball's that I've told you about—Fern Thorndyke and Kimball's attorney and stockbroker, Marcus Proctor—they hired a man to murder me. Last night it was Loi Yan's turn.

"I killed Kelvin and I left McGrath tied up over on the other side of the Sierra Nevada. I don't know where Fern Thorndyke and Marcus Proctor are at the moment, but it's more'n likely they're right here in town. I've been keeping an eye peeled for that pair. But I don't want to have to be on the lookout for that shady lady you're sheltering here at the mission."

"You mean Loi Yan."

"That's exactly who I mean. I came here to tell you that you'd best keep her under lock and key, else I'll go to the police and swear out a warrant for her arrest on a charge of attempted murder. I don't want her tailing me with another dagger up her sleeve or maybe even a gun next time. I told you I killed Kelvin when he threw down on me. I hope I don't have to kill Loi Yan. But I got to tell you, Roberta, I'll do whatever it takes to keep anybody—man or woman—from putting any holes in my hide."

Roberta, wringing her hands, moaned in obvious distress. "I can't keep Loi Yan under lock and key, as you put it, Luke."

"You can't? Why can't you?"

"She went out yesterday morning and she hasn't returned. Apparently, from what you say, she went to your hotel, where she waited for you and then after the uh, incident, she may have felt that she couldn't return here. Perhaps she feared your vengeance, and from what you've just said to me, she has good reason to do so."

Sutton heard the icy tone of Roberta's voice. "You're right. Loi Yan's got good reason to be wary of me, like I just told you."

"But surely you can understand her concern for her friend—for Ah Toy?"

"I can. What I can't understand is her pigsticking tricks. I tried to find Ah Toy and I'll keep on trying. So Loi Yan, she ought to be on my side, not against me."

"The girl is upset. Distraught, I daresay."

Sutton rose. "Well, what I think you'd best do when next you lay eyes on her is warn her to stay far away from me if she knows what's good for her."

Roberta also rose. "I promise you that I shall do my best to soothe her, to reassure her that you'll do whatever you can to find her friend. I'm sure I can persuade Loi Yan to be reasonable—if I see her again."

Roberta followed Sutton as he left the parlor and

headed for the door. When he reached it, she asked, "What are you going to do now, Luke?"

"I had me a run-in with that Buzzer Dunn fellow you told me about the last time we talked. I'm on my way to have another talk with him on account of how I never did get to find out whether or not he knows where I ought to go to put my paws on Kimball."

When no one answered Sutton's loud knock on the second-floor door of number 33 Pacific Street, above Shanghai Kelly's Saloon, he tried the door and found it locked. He knocked as loudly a second time, and when he still received no response, he stepped back, twisted his body, and rammed his shoulder against the door. It burst open, and he found himself on the threshold of a filthy room that was completely empty. The room had no closets and no window. Instead of a bed, there was a pallet of old rags lying in a rumpled heap on the floor. There was no place in the room where a man could hide.

Sutton turned on his heel, intending to head for the Cowboy's Rest, where he planned to question Lady Dora about Dunn's whereabouts, when he collided with a di-minutive Chinese man who was approaching Dunn's living quarters.

"Buzzer drunk one more time?" the unperturbed Chinese asked Sutton, grinning from ear to ear and pointing at the door. "He bust up door?"

"Who are you?"

"Dah Pa Tsin. You friend to Dunn?"

"I'm looking for him. You know him, I take it?" When Dah Pa Tsin nodded, his grin never wavering, Sutton continued, "Do you know where he is?"

"Dunn not here?"

"Nope. And I need to see him real bad."

"He got hot Chinese girl for you? Cocaine? Never mind. Both no good. You buy white pigeon ticket from Dah Pa Tsin. White pigeon ticket not give disease, not burn out brain." A Chinese lottery ticket appeared in Dah Pa Tsin's hand. He thrust it at Sutton. "Four bits cheap."

Sutton took the ticket, paid for it, and proceeded to check ten of the eighty Chinese characters printed on the ticket with a pencil handed to him by Dah Pa Tsin.

"Drawing later today," Dah Pa Tsin told him as Sutton gave the man the ticket he had marked. "Pigeons carry tickets from men like me to office of gambling chief. You catch five numbers of twenty drawn, you win two dollar. You catch six, you win twenty dollar. You catch seven, you win two hundred dollar. You catch—"

"I know how the lottery works," Sutton interrupted impatiently. "You came here to sell Dunn one of your lottery tickets?"

"Ah no! Not so! Dunn big gambler. He work for chief gambling man. Me work for Dunn. You buy maybe 'nother ticket? Take chance to win twice?"

"You don't know where Dunn is?"

"I know maybe."

"You do? Where is he then?"

"You buy five more my tickets?"

Sutton promptly bought five more tickets from Dah Pa Tsin, considering the bribe an inexpensive one as he did so. The Chinese beamed, beckoned, and then started down the stairs. Sutton followed him through the streets, neither man speaking until they turned right off Market Street onto Kearny Street, where Dah Pa Tsin halted and pointed to a dingy sign that hung above steps leading downward to a basement door, which had above it a sign bearing six Chinese characters.

"What's that say?" Sutton asked warily, pointing to the sign.

"*Kung in san tiu* mean Panta opium sold here. You come. Dunn sometime in here. He smoke dope. Dream sweet dreams. You come."

Sutton followed Dah Pa Tsin as he scampered down the stairs, and as he entered the smoky room beyond the door, he halted and coughed. He squinted down the dimly lighted passage ahead of him which was bordered by cubicles set into the smoke-charred walls. Pairs of drugged men lay facing each other in the cubicles on thin pallets, their heads resting on blocks of wood. Other men, most of them Chinese but some of them white, reclined on other pallets as they warmed their bamboo-stem pipes over the cut-glass lamp standing between them while simultaneously spearing small opium nuggets with the point of a thin wire poker, which they then also held over the flame of the lamp to cause them to swell to more than twice their size.

Sutton turned his attention away from the smokers to Dah Pa Tsin, who was hurrying down the passageway, darting from side to side to peer into the shadowy faces of the smokers. When Dah Pa Tsin beckoned to him, Sutton followed the man and then halted when Dah Pa Tsin did.

"Dunn not here," Dah Pa Tsin declared nonchalantly, and eased around Sutton, heading for the door.

"You sure?" Sutton asked as he made his way back along the passageway. He couldn't help coughing as a result of the room's oppressive air, so heavily laden with the stupefying fumes of the opium that was being smoked on all sides.

"We go Kwan Kung now."

"Hold on!" Sutton caught up with Dah Pa Tsin. "What's this Kwan Kung you're talking about now?"

"Dunn come this place sometime. But he not here now. So we go Kwan Kung. It place named for Chinese god of war. Play fan-tan there. Find Dunn there maybe so."

Later, as Sutton entered the gambling hall behind Dah Pa Tsin, he found the room a sharp contrast with the dingy opium den he had visited earlier. The gambling hall was brightly lighted and crowded with animated Chinese men who were packed shoulder-to-shoulder at the gaming tables.

"Good name for this place, Kwan Kung," Dah Pa Tsin declared as he and Sutton stopped at a fan-tan table. "Gambling like war. Players fight house to win. Not with sword but—look."

Sutton looked at the box Dah Pa Tsin had pointed out to him, which contained Chinese brass coins and small pieces of orange peel.

"Owner of house from Canton Province," Dah Pa Tsin told Sutton. "He put orange peel in fan-tan box. Orange color of good omen. In Canton sometimes babies washed in orange juice when born so fortune will come to child. Look!"

Sutton looked at the plain whitewashed walls Dah Pa Tsin had just pointed out to him.

"White is Chinese color of mourning. Also of robes worn by dead. House make walls white to make players lose. Also, orange peel in fan-tan boxes to bring good fortune to house. Is war here, yes?"

Sutton nodded absently and scanned the crowd, searching for a glimpse of Buzzer Dunn.

"You no worry," Dah Pa Tsin told him. "I go find

Dunn. You stay. Play fan-tan, yes? No worry. I come back."

As Dah Pa Tsin promptly disappeared in the crowd, Sutton turned and looked down at the fan-tan table and the eighteen-inch square that was painted on its wooden surface. He watched the dealer then, and when the man tossed a handful of brass coins onto the table, he stared hard at them, trying to count them, knowing that the object of the game was for the player to try to guess correctly how many coins—one, two, three, or more—would remain when the total number of coins had been divided by four.

The dealer swiftly clapped a shallow metal cover, not unlike one used to cover a frying pan, over the coins.

Sutton, as the men around him chattered in Chinese and eagerly placed their bets on the tabletop square's sides that were numbered one, two, three, and zero, put a dollar on the side numbered two.

The betting continued for some time, and then when it finally ended, the dealer lifted the cover to reveal the coins. Then, using a chopstick, he proceeded to separate the coins he had tossed onto the table into neat groups of four. When he had finished doing so, a lone coin remained.

Sutton shrugged off his loss and again surveyed the crowd in the gambling hall. He saw no sign of Dunn or of Dah Pa Tsin either. But then, just as he was about to make his way toward the rear of the huge room, he heard a shrill cry behind him and turned to see Dah Pa Tsin fall to the floor as Dunn shoved him out of his way, turned, and headed for the front door. Sutton pushed his way through the crowd and past the floored Dah Pa Tsin, who looked up at him with an expression of fear on his face. He silently cursed his slow progress through the almost unyielding mass of bodies. He cursed again as he momentarily lost sight of Dunn but then saw the man again as Dunn also fought his way through the crowded room toward the door that led to the street outside.

Sutton reached the door moments after Dunn had gone racing through it. He emerged from the stuffy gambling room and looked up and down the street, his fists clenched at his sides.

There!

He tore down the street after Dunn, whom he had spotted just before the fleeing man turned a corner and was lost to sight. When Sutton turned the same corner, he found Dunn desperately trying to scale a wooden wall at the end of a dark alley. Seconds later he was at the wall and the fingers of both of his hands closed around Dunn's ankles. He jerked on them while Dunn, hanging on to the top of the fence, tried to kick him in the face. Sutton, still holding tightly to Dunn's right ankle with his right hand, reached up with his left, seized the man's belt, and pulled him down to the ground.

Dunn spun around, and Sutton stepped back when he saw the knife in the man's hand that seemed to have materialized out of the empty air. As Dunn lunged at him, Sutton's gun cleared leather and he fired. His shot missed the knife which had been his intended target and hit Dunn's right hand.

Dunn screamed, a high-pitched despairing sound. He dropped his knife, seized the wrist of his wounded hand, and continued howling in agony as blood spurted from it.

"You need a doctor," Sutton muttered, his gun now leveled at Dunn's chest. "You don't get one, you'll bleed to death, Dunn."

As Dunn took an unsteady step in the direction of the

alley's mouth, Sutton intercepted him and pressed the barrel of his .45 against the wounded man's chest.

"Stay put, Dunn."

"Got to—doctor."

"You're not going anyplace till you tell me what you know about Ted Kimball."

Dunn whimpered. "Let me go. I'm bleeding to death."

"I know you know where Kimball's holed up," Sutton stated bluntly, having decided to bluff Dunn. "You tell me where he's at, and I'll let you go find a doctor to patch you up."

"Damn that Dah Pa Tsin!" Dunn cried, beginning to weep. "When I saw who that stupid Celestial had brought to me—I should have killed him on the spot instead of just knocking the son of a bitch down."

"Dunn, let's you and me stick to the subject at hand. Which happens to be Ted Kimball."

"Let me go! Look!" Dunn held up his bleeding hand, which he was still clutching at the wrist. "Please—"

"Kimball. Where is he?"

"She'll kill me if I tell!"

"Who will?"

"Lady Dora."

"*I'll* kill you if you *don't* tell," Sutton assured Dunn, elation surging through him as he realized that his bluff had worked. "I just might put one more bullet into you— into your uncooperative heart this time."

"Lady Dora's hiding him."

"How'd Kimball and the likes of that shanghaiing Lady Dora get mixed up together?"

"He came to the Barbary Coast and asked me who could help him hide out from the law. I took him to Lady Dora. He told her he was wanted for murder in Virginia City. She said she'd hide him. And hide him she did. But she's blackmailing him. She told him she'll turn him in to the San Francisco police the minute he stops paying her a hundred dollars a day."

"Where is Kimball?"

"In the basement underneath a crib at 210 Stouts Alley in Chinatown. Now that I've told you—please—can I go now?"

Sutton leathered his gun, and as if his action had been a signal, Dunn went racing past him and out of the alley.

Sutton retraced his steps and headed for 210 Stouts Alley.

"China girl nice. You come inside, please?"

Sutton stopped in front of the door of the crib in Stouts Alley, which had a barred window behind which stood a weary-looking young Chinese woman.

She disappeared and was replaced by another woman who reached through the bars and beckoned to Sutton, a tired smile on her forlorn face. In a singsong voice, she cried, "Two bittee lookee, flo bittee feelee, six bittee doee."

Sutton went down the garbage-strewn steps that led to the basement and, without bothering to knock, tried the door he found there. It was locked, as he had expected it would be. He hammered on it with his fist but received no response. He climbed back up the stairs and stood on the landing surveying the alley as the woman beside him at her barred window wheedled, "You come inside to nice China girl, please? Your father, he just go out."

Sutton, smiling at the preposterous statement the woman had just made, chose a recessed doorway on one side of it as the place where he would wait and watch for Kimball. Once ensconced in it, he leaned back, wondering how long he would have to wait. Would Kimball put in an appearance? If so, when? Was the man still using the basement hideout? Was he maybe inside it at this very moment?

Sutton knew no answers to his questions. He resigned himself to waiting. To waiting a long time if necessary.

It was midafternoon when he, barely conscious now of the monotonous voice of the most recent Chinese woman to stand behind the barred window of the crib as she recited her tawdry list of services and prices, caught sight of a familiar face in the crowd that was jamming Stouts Alley.

He straightened, his heartbeat quickening, as he stared at the man who was hurrying down the alley and occasionally glancing back over his shoulder as if he thought —or feared—he was being pursued.

Sutton continued staring at Theodore Kimball, whom he had recognized from the man's picture that was on the dodger he had in his pocket. When Kimball darted down the steps next to the crib's entrance, he moved out after the man.

When he reached the top of the stairs, Kimball was hurriedly unlocking the door below. Sutton bounded down the steps, taking them two and three at a time, and as Kimball opened the door, he shoved his quarry inside the dark room beyond the door and slammed it shut behind him.

"Light a lamp, Kimball!" Moments later, when yellow lamplight flared in the dingy low-ceilinged room, he said, "Kimball, you sure are a hard man to find."

"Who—" Kimball breathed nervously and then: "Who are you?"

"Name's Luke Sutton. I guess you could call me a bounty hunter."

Kimball's eyes widened. He cried out as the wooden

match he was holding burned his fingers and went out. He dropped it and repeated, "Bounty hunter," in a strangled voice.

"I've come to take you back to Virginia City to stand trial for the murder of Dade McGrath."

Kimball slumped down in a wooden chair, his arms hanging listlessly at his sides, his head bent, and his eyes fixed on the bare floor.

Sutton studied him, noting the unruly shock of brown hair which tended to fall down upon his broad forehead, his square and heavily stubbled chin, his almost rail-thin frame. He doesn't look like a murderer, Sutton thought. He doesn't look like a lawyer either, for that matter. He could pass for a preacher.

Kimball looked up at Sutton, who saw despair in the man's amber eyes. "I didn't kill Dade McGrath," he said in a low voice.

"You stand accused by the law of doing just that. A judge and jury'll decide whether you did or not." Sutton's hand dropped to the butt of his gun. "Before we leave here, Kimball, I've got me a question to put to you. Where's Ah Toy?"

"Ah Toy," Kimball repeated lifelessly. "You know her?"

Sutton described his encounter with Ming Long of the Kwong Dock tong and then told Kimball about the visit that Loi Yan had paid him. "Loi Yan said she reckons Ah Toy's gone back to the place you set up for her when you first got her away from Ming Long. Only Loi Yan doesn't know where that someplace is nor, as I understand it, does anybody else excepting you."

Kimball rose to his feet with a mournful sigh. "It's—" He gasped as the basement door suddenly flew open. He stepped back, his right hand stretched out in front of him as if he were trying to ward off a blow.

Sutton, who had spun around toward the door at the sound of Kimball's startled gasp, his hand on his gun butt, found himself confronting Buzzer Dunn, who was standing and smiling in the doorway. Flanking him were two men, both of whom held revolvers in their hands.

Dunn held up his bandaged hand and then shook it at Sutton. "I figured I might find you here," he muttered. "I hoped to hell I would, I can tell you that, because I got a score to settle with you, Sutton."

Sutton swiftly unleathered his gun, but before he could fire, the man on Dunn's left shot the .45 out of his hand.

"Good shooting, Dex," Dunn crowed, his eyes glowing. "You," he barked and pointed at Kimball. "I got no quarrel with you. Get out of here!"

Kimball hesitated a moment and then scurried past Sutton, Dunn, and Dunn's two companions.

Sutton heard his footsteps as he fled from the room and up the stairs heading to Stouts Alley.

Dunn, in the doorway, smiled the smile of a snake. Pointing at Sutton, he said, "Shoot the son of a bitch, boys!"

SEVEN

Both men flanking Sutton squeezed their triggers, and flame, followed by smoke, poured forth from the barrels of their six-guns.

Sutton had thrown himself to the floor and both shots missed him. He had barely hit the floor when he was up on his knees and then up on his feet. As the man nearest to him again eared back the hammer of his revolver, he reached out and clamped his left hand around the gun's barrel, preventing his would-be assailant from firing.

He pulled the startled man toward him, jerked the gun out of his hand, and then threw him into Dunn, who staggered backward, striking the man beside him, and causing his companion's gun to go off as a result of the sudden collision.

Dunn's mouth opened, but no sound came from it as the man who had just accidentally shot him stared at him, a shocked and uncertain expression on his face, smoke wisping up from the lowered barrel of his gun. Dunn gave a tortured groan as his knees began to give way under him. The man who had shot him stood paralyzed, staring in awe as a bubbly red froth slid slowly out of Dunn's mouth and began to run down his chin.

Sutton, out of the corner of his eye, caught movement on his right. He turned sharply to find the man he had earlier disarmed stoop and scoop up the sheriff's Colt that had been shot out of his own hand earlier. As the man, down on one knee with Sutton's gun gripped in both of his hands, cocked it, Sutton hurled the gun that he had taken from him earlier. It struck the man's chin, causing bone to snap and the man's scream to resound in the room. Sutton moved in on the still-kneeling man and kicked the .45 out of his hand.

Then, after retrieving both guns, he turned back to face the gunman who had shot Dunn and who was now gazing down in a dazed fashion at Dunn's obviously lifeless body that was lying on the floor at his feet. Slowly, the man looked up. As slowly his gun rose. He held it there a dreamy moment, staring as if puzzled at Sutton.

Sutton, an instant before the man could fire at him, fired both of the guns he held in his hands, putting two bullets in his would-be killer's brain.

And then, as the man he had just been forced to kill in self-defense dropped his gun, pitched forward, and fell facedown on the floor, Sutton was struck from behind by a pair of fists that slammed against the base of his skull. The savage attack knocked him to his knees and caused his vision to blur badly. As he struggled to rise, he was kicked in the small of the back. He fell, rolled over, looked up, and saw the other man, who had retrieved the gun that had been dropped by the man just shot to death.

Lying on his back, a vision of his deadly adversary flickering before his still-blurry eyes, Sutton knew with a sad certainty what he was going to do—what he had to do. He fired two shots in swift succession. Both buried themselves in the gut of the malevolently leering man who was looming over him. As the man fell forward, Sutton rolled out of the way. The man he had killed crashed to the floor next to him. He slowly got to his feet, holstered his .45, and tossed the gun that had belonged to one of his attackers on the unmade bed. Drawing a deep

breath and then letting it out, he turned and made his
way out of Kimball's room, which had become Death's
bloody domain.

Sutton strode purposefully through the streets of San
Francisco toward his destination, thoughts swarming
through his mind. He was barely conscious of the crowd
of people through which he moved. He hardly noticed
the glow of the water in the bay that was being made
brassy by the afternoon sun.

Damn Dunn, he thought, for letting Kimball get away
from me. And damn Kimball for getting away, he
thought. I had my hands on the man and then Dunn and
his bully boys— He shoved his thoughts aside. Spilled
milk. No use shedding any tears over what had happened. The thing to do now is to find Kimball again, he
told himself.

His expression became grim. Find Kimball. Sure. But
how? And where? Well, he thought, I'm already on my
way to start trailing the man again. Maybe I'll have me a
little bit of luck. Maybe I can catch hold of Kimball before anybody else does. Anybody like Loi Yan or Ming
Long, for example, he thought uneasily.

When he reached the Cowboy's Rest, he entered the
nearly empty saloon. Two men sat at a table near the
entrance, nursing flat beers in a silence as flat. Near the
bar sat a man with his arms folded on the table in front of
him, his head resting on them as he alternately snored
and mumbled incoherently to himself. Lady Dora, behind the bar, was whistling through her teeth as she
dried wet glasses with a dirty rag.

Sutton went up to the bar and, with no preamble or
any acknowledgment of Lady Dora's failed attempt to
shanghai him at their first meeting, said flatly, "I'm look-

ing for Ted Kimball and I think you just might know where he is."

Lady Dora peered at Sutton through uneasy eyes for a long moment, and then apparently deciding that he meant her no harm, she tried a smile. "Have a drink. On the house."

Sutton ignored the glass she filled and placed in front of him on the mahogany bar. "Ted Kimball," he repeated. "Where is he?"

"I don't know. Or care." Lady Dora turned her attention to the glasses she had been polishing, studiously holding one up and squinting at it.

"You were hiding him in a basement underneath a Chinese whorehouse in Stouts Alley."

"How did you—" Lady Dora's lips clamped shut in a grim line as she stared balefully at Sutton.

"I found Kimball in Stouts Alley with the help of Buzzer Dunn but then Dunn found the both of us in Stouts Alley and there was some trouble. During it Dunn and two of his friends got themselves killed and Kimball flew the coop."

"Buzzer's dead?"

Sutton nodded.

"You killed him?"

Sutton nodded again.

Lady Dora stepped back from the bar.

"I know you know that Kimball's wanted for murder in Virginia City," Sutton stated bluntly. "That's why you were making him pay you a hundred dollars a day for that filthy hole he'd been living in."

Lady Dora frowned. "How'd you know that?"

"Dunn told me, that's how I knew."

"That bastard! Buzzer never could keep his mouth shut about business matters." Lady Dora's features gradually relaxed. "Well, after all, a lady has to earn her keep," she declared almost jauntily.

"No lady would kick a man when he's down, which is what you and your hundred-dollars-a-day rent was doing to Ted Kimball. Now, why don't you just tell me where to find him?"

Lady Dora turned away from Sutton and frowned. "What do you want, Wickers?"

Sutton glanced at the aged and ragged derelict who had appeared beside him, and he recognized the man as the one who had been half asleep at a nearby table when he had entered the saloon.

"Lady Dora, my dear," the man named Wickers whined. "I'm so thirsty my gullet thinks I'm living in the Sonoran Desert."

"Get out of here, Wickers," Lady Dora ordered.

"I will, my dear, I surely will. But first—couldn't you see your way clear to give me a drink—just one, mind you—on credit until I get my next paycheck?"

Lady Dora stared with undisguised scorn at Wickers and harrumphed her disbelief and indignation. "Your next paycheck indeed! You haven't worked in years, you old reprobate. And as far as credit goes—you've not got a cent's worth in the Cowboy's Rest, you haven't. Now haul your freight before I come out from behind this bar and put your lights out for you."

Wickers nervously plucked at Sutton's arm. "She's a hard one, Lady Dora is. But you, sir—I can see you have kind eyes and that means—oh, how I hope it means—that you also have a kind heart. Won't you take pity on a man who's down and out and buy him a drink?"

"What'll it be, Wickers?" Sutton asked, digging into his pocket and then tossing a coin on the bar.

"Whiskey, Lady Dora!" cried Wickers gleefully, both

of his hands gripping the bar, both of his eyes fixed on the coin Sutton had tossed on the bar. "Make it a double."

"Where's Kimball?" Sutton asked Lady Dora.

"I already told you I don't know—or care—where he is!" Lady Dora snapped as she poured Wickers' drink.

"Look," Sutton began in what he hoped was a reasonable tone despite his growing irritation with Lady Dora. "I—"

"To your health, kind sir," Wickers said to Sutton as he raised his glass to his lips. "I do thank you for the libation."

"Enjoy it, old-timer," Sutton said absently. Then to Lady Dora: "I found out that Kimball came here to the Barbary Coast on account of he thought it would be a good place for him to drop out of sight. He came here specifically, I happen to know, to see Buzzer Dunn, whom he knew because he had once represented Dunn in a legal matter. Dunn turned Kimball over to you—probably for a cut of whatever deal Kimball and you could come up with—and you went and set Kimball up in that hideout in Stouts Alley."

Wickers ostentatiously placed his empty glass on the bar and glanced hopefully at Sutton, who ignored him. Fatalistically shrugging his shoulders and thrusting his hands into his pockets, Wickers plopped down at his table behind Sutton, his expression morose.

"The way I see it," Sutton continued, addressing Lady Dora, "Kimball would have come running right back here to you now that his cover's been blown to get you to set him up someplace else. Was he here?"

Lady Dora looked down at the floor. She sighed. Then, meeting Sutton's steady gaze, she said, "I guess there's no use playing ring-around-the-rosy with you anymore. I'll level with you. I might as well.

"Kimball did come here. He told me about you being a bounty hunter. He told me Buzzer had come to Stouts Alley to kill you and that Buzzer had ordered him to hightail it out of the place. When I heard Kimball's story, I told him I didn't want any trouble. I told him I was taking a risk when I hid him in the first place. And now that he had a bounty hunter on his trail, I told him I didn't want anything more to do with him. And now here you are trying to make trouble for me."

"How'd Kimball take what you had to tell him?"

"He was upset. He pleaded with me. He said he had no place else to go. I told him to beat it. He did."

Sutton hesitated. Was Lady Dora telling him the truth? He didn't know, couldn't be sure. He turned and almost fell over Wickers' legs, which were sprawled out behind him.

Wickers withdrew his legs and Sutton left the Cowboy's Rest. He stood outside for a moment, debating his next move.

"Kind sir."

He turned to find Wickers sidling up to him. "Lady Dora lies," Wickers said slyly with a wicked grin, "the way some women lead men on. Real easy."

"What are you talking about, old-timer?" Sutton asked hopefully. "Are you claiming Lady Dora lied to me just now?"

"About the fellow you mentioned named Kimball. Yep, she did. I've been in the Cowboy's Rest since it opened up early this morning, and this fellow named Kimball, he came in a while ago—I heard her call him by name."

"Go on," Sutton urged. "What happened?"

Wickers gave Sutton an off-center grin. "That Lady Dora—she's a mean old harridan, that she is. Wouldn't give me a drink—but you, you were kind to me, buying me that drink I needed so badly. So I thought I'd return the favor you did me and get back at Lady Dora all at the same time."

Wickers looked up and down the street and then, taking Sutton by the arm, drew him away from the entrance to the Cowboy's Rest. "Lady Dora," he confided in a whisper, "has this button behind the bar. When she presses it, it releases a spring in a trapdoor she's got set in the floor at the end of the bar. When she does that, any man standing on that spot is dropped down into her basement. Then the enterprising Lady Dora turns over the men she drops down through her trapdoor to a pair of thugs for a hefty fee per head. The thugs, they then sell the unfortunate fellows as crewmen and—"

"I know Lady Dora's in the business of shanghaiing men," Sutton interrupted. "But what about Kimball?"

Wickers gave Sutton a sly smile. "She shanghaied him."

"When?"

"Not more than an hour before you showed up at the Cowboy's Rest. She lied to you about him. I was there and I saw him get himself shanghaied, and I'm willing to wager that the unfortunate Mr. Kimball is already aboard the *Mary Malone* that lies anchored in the bay while her captain tries to round up a full crew by hook or by crook. Mostly by crook, it looks like to me."

Sutton came up with a fast five dollars in hard money which he handed to Wickers. "I'm much obliged to you, old-timer."

"I'm much obliged to you, young fella!" Wickers called

out ecstatically to Sutton, who was hurrying away and heading for the docks.

As soon as Sutton arrived at the docks, he hired a fishing boat captain to take him out to the *Mary Malone*.

"She's a bad ship," the captain remarked as he stood with Sutton in the wheelhouse of his small vessel. "What you want with her's none of my business, but maybe you won't mind a friendly word of warning. Watch your step once you've boarded her."

Sutton nodded and the rest of the journey was completed in silence.

Minutes later, when the fishing boat came within sight of the *Mary Malone*, still riding at anchor in the bay, Sutton pointed and said, "Pull up on her port side. I'll climb the Jacob's ladder. Wait for me. I'll be back—me and another man will be—just as fast as I can manage it."

The captain gave him a skeptical glance but said nothing. As the fishing boat pulled up alongside the *Mary Malone*, Sutton went out on deck and then began to climb the Jacob's ladder.

When he emerged on the *Mary Malone*'s deck, he blinked in the blinding glare of the setting sun reflected off the water. Then, squinting, he scanned the faces of the few men working on the deck. None was Kimball. He strode across the deck, stepping over coiled lines and skirting open hatchways as he headed for the passageway that led below decks. Just as he reached it, the winch sprang into raucous life as it began to draw up the anchor.

He reached for the doorknob, and as he did so, the door opened and he found himself confronting the captain of the *Mary Malone*.

The captain's face froze. "You!" he muttered in an alarmed voice.

Sutton seized the man by the throat and pushed him back beyond the door. Closing the door behind him, he muttered, "I've come for a man named Kimball. Where've you got him?"

The captain shook his head, whether to deny knowledge of Kimball's whereabouts or simply to try to deny what was happening to him, Sutton wasn't sure. "Answer up, captain. You don't, I'll send you head over heels down those steps behind you. Now, where's Kimball?"

"He put up a fight when he was brought aboard a little while ago. I had him put in irons. He's down in the hold."

"Take me to him."

The captain nodded nervously and led Sutton out onto the deck.

"You make one wrong move," Sutton warned him, "and my gun'll let light through you. You got that?"

The captain nodded as nervously a second time and led the way to an open hatch. "Down there."

"Let's go." Sutton let the captain climb down the ladder that led to the hold first, and then he quickly followed.

"I'll light a lantern," the captain volunteered as he and Sutton stood in the hold that was only faintly illuminated by the fading sunlight falling through the open hatch.

When the lantern flared into life, Sutton found himself confronting Kimball, who was sitting on the deck of the hold, his ankles in chains and his wrists shackled to eyebolts set in the hold's bulkhead above his head.

Kimball closed his eyes against the lantern's light that was apparently blinding him.

"Set him free," Sutton ordered the captain, who went to Kimball, took a ring of keys from his pocket, knelt down, and began to unlock Kimball's chains.

Kimball opened his eyes and stared up at Sutton. "How did you know where to find me?" he asked in a dull voice.

"You don't sound glad to see me, Kimball," Sutton observed. "You should be though, considering I'm here to get you out of the fix you've gone and got yourself into."

The captain rose and stepped back, the long chains that had imprisoned Kimball dangling from his right hand.

Sutton stepped around the captain, bent down, and helped Kimball get to his feet. "I've got a boat waiting to take us ashore. Let's go."

As Kimball, partially supported by Sutton, took a step toward the ladder that led to the deck, he suddenly sagged.

Sutton put one arm around his waist and draped the man's right arm over his shoulder. Gripping Kimball's wrist in his right hand, be began to ease the man toward the ladder.

He never made it.

The captain swung the chains in his hand and they struck Sutton's body with bone-shattering force, bowling him over. He lost his hold on Kimball and hit the deck. As he did so, he heard Kimball let out an alarmed cry. He turned, his arm raised to shield his face, and saw two things. Kimball was staggering toward the ladder leading to the upper deck and the captain, ignoring Kimball, was raising his chains.

As the chains arced upward through the air, and Kimball clumsily climbed the ladder and then emerged on

the deck above, one of them struck the lantern the captain had lighted earlier, shattering it.

Blazing coal oil spilled from the lantern in a shower of
bright sparks, and when the gobbets of airborne oil
splashed against the wooden bulkheads and deck, they set
them on fire.

The chains in the captain's hand had almost completed
their deadly arc when Sutton's gun cleared leather. But
before he could cock his Colt and fire—before he could
even manage to roll out of the way of the deadly descend-
ing iron—the chains struck him, knocking the gun from
his hand, which slid across the deck, and leaving a legacy
of agony in their wake.

He lost consciousness, but another savage blow of the
chains brought it—and awful pain—back to him. He felt
himself slipping, felt himself sliding back down into that
deep black place where oblivion lived, the pit from
which he had just emerged. There once again he drifted
in impenetrable darkness with pain his only companion,
and he thought he heard men crying out to one another.
To him the frantic cries sounded like the voices of the
doomed.

Kimball suddenly appeared and scampered mockingly
through Sutton's mind. He reached out to seize the man
but Kimball eluded him and went dancing and prancing
down an endless street that was bordered not by shops
but by red walls of flickering fire. He turned and, puffing
up his cheeks, blew a blast of fiery breath, bringing sweat
to Sutton's face and body, both of which were soon
drenched with it. He tried to run after the gamboling
Kimball, who was dancing a taunting gavotte amid the
flames, but he found he could not move. He tried to
shout Kimball's name, tried to persuade the man to come
back to him and to become his prisoner once again, but

Kimball only laughed giddily and then, amid a burst of sparks, shot upward into the distant sky and disappeared from sight.

Sutton tried to pursue Kimball and his desperate trying brought consciousness rushing back to him, a hot flood. He opened his eyes and, through thick clouds of smoke, saw his bent fingers clawing the rough wooden deck. He saw the flames that were consuming the bulkheads, the ship's crated cargo, the deck underfoot.

Sutton, his strong will to survive whipping him mercilessly into life-saving action, managed to get to his feet. He stood there in the smoky center of the holocaust, swaying unsteadily, his eyes on the square piece of the night sky, bright with cold stars, that was visible through the open hatch overhead. He lowered his eyes to the ladder that led up to the hatch and the main deck. Flames had found it and were flickering almost gaily on some of its rungs and on one of its uprights.

Sutton retrieved his gun, holstered it, and staggered toward the ladder. The pain that had been sired throughout most of his body by the captain's merciless chains ripped through him, threatening to throw him. But he forced himself to put one unsteady foot in front of the other as he kept his eyes on the ladder that led to the world above the inferno in which he found himself as heat from the flames around him squeezed sweat from his face and body.

Seven, eight . . .

He kept counting his steps as he came closer to the ladder that offered him a way—the only way—out of the hell that the hold had become.

Ten . . .

He took off his hat and used it to beat back the thick smoke that was filling the hold. He moved on and then

let out a guttural cry as the hair on the left side of his
head suddenly flared into flame. He quickly beat to death
with his hat the flames that had so briefly haloed his
head. Clapping his hat back on his head and breathing
hard, he reached for the ladder with both hands. He put
one boot on its partially charred lowest rung.

The rung snapped.

He put his boot on the next highest rung and was
about to begin his climb toward the hatch overhead
when the flames that were eating into the end of the
ladder's uprights directly above his head suddenly flared
wildly and the ladder gave way and fell flaming down to
the deck of the hold.

Sutton, as he leaped backward out of its fiery way and
slapped away sparks and small fragments of burning debris that had once been part of the ladder, fought hard
against his own pain and the panic that was rising within
him like a devastating tide. He rubbed both his eyes,
which the smoke was causing to tear, with his fists, and
then he made a dash for the few crates of cargo that were
so far untouched by the flames. Putting his shoulder behind a pile that was several crates high, he managed to
slide them very slowly along the deck. He kept straining
against them, easing them along the deck inch by slow
inch until at last they stood directly below the open
hatch. Then, turning, he toppled another large pile of
crates and hurriedly climbed up on top of one of them.
By stretching as far as he could, he managed to grip the
top of the uppermost crate in the pile he had placed below the hatch. His boots scrabbled against the sides of
the crates as he painstakingly hauled himself up and then
climbed on top of the uppermost crate. He lay face down
upon it, panting and fighting for breath.

He coughed violently as acrid smoke billowed up

around him and then got first to his hands and knees and then to his feet. He reached up and hauled himself up and onto the deserted deck. He stood alone in the silent night gulping cool air into his lungs as tears caused by the searing smoke from the fire in the hold flowed from his eyes. He was seized by a gut-wrenching fit of coughing that caused him to double over. When it finally ended, he straightened, glanced over his shoulder at the flames that were now spouting up like red geysers through the open hatch, and then headed for the side of the ship.

He looked down. The fishing boat that had brought him to the *Mary Malone* was nowhere in sight. He looked out across the bay. No other ships were visible anywhere on its placid surface. The captain and the crew of the *Mary Malone*—Kimball too, apparently—had obviously abandoned the doomed ship. By way of the fishing boat? By swimming ashore? He had no way of knowing.

He pulled off his boots, tied them together with his bandanna, and hung them around his neck. He took off his hat, placed it between his teeth, and climbed up on the deck rail. He dived from it, his body slicing into the water of the bay below him like a blade. He came up fast and turned, treading water, until he was facing the shore. A moment later he was swimming toward it, his eyes fixed on the distant lights of San Francisco which glittered like jewels that someone had sprinkled along the coast and the hills directly above it.

Sutton lay sprawled facedown on his bed in his room in the Sailors' Haven Hotel, fully clothed, sound asleep, and blissfully unaware of the sounds being made by someone who was knocking urgently on his door.

He drifted in a sweet dream of clover-filled fields

where he and a woman named Elizabeth, who was no longer lost to him, roamed happily hand in hand.

"Luke!"

The woman's voice that had called his name frightened his dreamed Elizabeth and, as she fled from him, he awoke with a feeling of having been badly cheated in a way he could not define by someone he could not name.

"Luke! Open the door! *Please, Luke!*"

He got up, feeling groggy, and made his way to the door which he unlocked and opened. "Roberta!"

She brushed past him into the room. Then, turning to face him as he closed the door, she said, "I just spoke to the room clerk downstairs and he told me you had come back to your room just before dawn this morning and that you hadn't left since. I came here to the hotel—I had to know, Luke, if you were all right. I feared—I thought —oh, I'm so glad you escaped from that ship!"

"You know about the *Mary Malone* burning up?" he asked, surprised at her knowledge.

"Ted told me."

"Kimball told you? You've seen him?"

Roberta nodded and then sat down in a chair by the window. "Your clothes—they're all wet. You should put on dry clothes, Luke, so that you don't catch a chill."

"I had to swim ashore from the *Mary Malone,*" he told her as he sat down on the edge of the bed. "By the time I got back here, I was bushed. I felt like I'd just built a barn in record time all by myself. *Two* barns."

"Ted told me what happened in the hold of the *Mary Malone.* He said he jumped overboard only a moment after he had escaped from the hold. He also swam to shore, and it wasn't until he got there, he said, that he realized the ship was on fire. He said he didn't know if you—if anyone—had been able to escape from the *Mary Malone*. I'm glad you did, Luke."

"What else did Kimball have to say to you?"

Roberta sighed, a forlorn sound. "He told me about Lady Dora and how she had at first hidden and later shanghaied him because he was becoming too much trouble for her—and about you. I asked him how I could help him, and he told me there was no way I—or anyone else, for that matter—could help him now.

"I pleaded with him to turn himself in. Either to you or to the authorities in Virginia City. I pointed out that there might have been extenuating circumstances involved when he murdered Mr. Dade McGrath."

Sutton got up from the bed and went to the open window, where he stared out over the overhang for a moment before turning back to Roberta and asking, "What'd he have to say to that suggestion of yours?"

"He just shook his head." Roberta looked down at her hands, which were twisting nervously in her lap, and then up again at Sutton. "Isn't it possible that a court would understand that what Ted did—that it was a rash act, not premeditated murder? If they did, wouldn't they be liable to be lenient in sentencing him? I mean they wouldn't—they couldn't, could they—sentence him to hang for what he did, given the circumstances of the crime?"

"I've got no good answers to give you, Roberta." Sutton impaled her with his steady gaze. "I know this is none of my business but—"

She waited expectantly.

"How come you're fretting so about Kimball and what happens to him? He's already got himself a woman—Fern Thorndyke, whom he was trying to protect when he killed Dade McGrath. From what I've heard, they were fixing to tie the knot."

"I know about Miss Thorndyke. I knew even before you mentioned her name to me the day we first met. Ted told me all about her. He never knew that I—men are so blind about certain things."

"He didn't know you'd fallen in love with him? Is that what you were fixing to say?"

"Yes. Ted thought—he still thinks—I'm just a good friend of his. I suppose it doesn't matter. What does matter"—Roberta looked up at Sutton in an almost defiant manner—"is that I want to do all I can to help him. I have to. When a woman feels the way I do about a man, she has no other choice if she is to be true to herself and what she feels."

"Where's Kimball now?" he asked, not sure that he would receive an answer to his question or, if he did receive one, whether it would be a truthful one.

"He said he was going to a cabin he built some time ago in the Sierra Nevada Mountains. He said he didn't want to leave San Francisco because he was supposed to meet Miss Thorndyke at his boardinghouse, but he had not been able to do so because the police were watching it as well as his office building. They had been doing so, he told me, ever since he returned to San Francisco, which is why he has been unable to meet Miss Thorndyke. And that is also why he was forced to go to Mr. Dunn on the Barbary Coast in the hope of finding a safe place to hide."

"Did he tell you where this cabin of his is?"

"Not exactly, no, he didn't. But he did say it was on the southern bank of the Stanislaus River just this side of the Sonora Pass." Roberta hesitated a moment. "You're going after him?"

"I am. You knew I would. That's why you came here to tell me about Kimball coming to call on you."

She nodded. "But now—now I don't know if I've done the right thing or not. I'm so afraid I might have done the wrong thing in coming here to you as I've done."

Sutton said nothing, knowing there was nothing he could say that would banish Roberta's misgivings.

She rose and went to the door. Then, turning back to face him, she said, "I was so upset by Ted's visit that I completely forgot to ask him where Ah Toy was—if he knew where she was. And now it's too late to ask him."

"I'll ask him once I catch up with him."

"I hope—" Roberta began, but she never did tell Sutton what it was that she hoped. Instead, she turned and hurriedly left the room.

He stood staring at the door she had closed behind her, fairly certain that he knew what it was that she had been about to say. She hopes I'll find Kimball, he thought. She hopes, once I get him back to Virginia City, that a jury'll go easy on him. That, he thought, must be what folks mean when they talk about love. He found himself envying Kimball, because the man had managed to have two lovely women fall in love with him. And one of them, he thought—Fern Thorndyke—had even lied to the law at first to keep Kimball from being suspected of the murder of Dade McGrath. And the other one—well, Roberta Pritchard's got her hopes, he thought, however outright foolish those hopes of hers might be.

The sudden harsh sound of a heavy footfall in the room behind him caused Sutton to spin around, his hand going for his gun.

"Don't touch that gun!" ordered the armed man facing him who had just climbed through the open window into the room.

Sutton's hand eased away from his .45 as he stared at Lorne McGrath, the brother of Dade McGrath, whom he had last seen in the Sierra Nevada Mountains, where McGrath had tried to kill him with the same Smith & Wesson revolver he was now aiming at him again.

EIGHT

"You're like a bad penny," Sutton told McGrath as he stared at the revolver in the man's hand. "You keep turning up."

"I told you I'd come after you," McGrath muttered.

"How'd you find me?"

"After I was freed by a deer hunter who found me all tied up where you left me in the mountains, I came straight here to San Francisco. Since I arrived, I've been hunting two men. Ted Kimball. And you. Finding you was relatively easy although somewhat time-consuming. I simply checked hotels in town until I came to this one, where you were registered. I staked the place out, and when I saw you standing in the window a little while ago —well, Sutton, here I am." McGrath's finger tightened on the trigger of his gun. "I had less luck finding Kimball, I must confess. No luck at all, as a matter of fact. So it was fortuitous that I heard the young lady who just visited you tell you— I hope you don't mind the fact that I was eavesdropping on your conversation, Sutton, while I waited outside on the overhang for the lady to leave. It was my good fortune to hear her tell you that Kimball had gone to a cabin of his on the Stanislaus River. That was a totally unexpected benefit resulting from my efforts to get to you before you could get to Kimball."

Sutton took a step toward the chair that sat next to the table near the door.

"Hold it, Sutton!" McGrath barked.

Sutton kept moving, his back to McGrath now, his body tense. He slowly sat down in the chair, his right arm thrust out at his side and nowhere near his gun. Facing McGrath once again, he said, "If you're bound and determined to shoot me, well, I reckon you can do it just as easy with me sitting down as standing."

"I can," McGrath said, a smile spreading across his pale face. His black eyes narrowed in anticipation as he continued staring hard at Sutton.

As McGrath's finger began to draw back the trigger of his .44, Sutton, in one swift movement, seized and up-ended the wooden table next to his chair. He was holding it out in front of him, its four legs aimed at McGrath, when the man's shot exploded in the room.

McGrath's bullet buried itself in the underside of the table's top, sending splinters flying in every direction. Before McGrath could fire a second time, Sutton lunged forward. Holding the table in the manner of an animal trainer, he used it to knock the gun from McGrath's hand, and then he pinned the man against the wall, two legs of the table on either side of McGrath's body.

McGrath, his arms pinioned beside his body, squirmed first one way then the other as he sought to break free of his four-legged prison.

Sutton suddenly dropped the table while simultaneously drawing his Colt. "You and me, McGrath, we're going downstairs to where I can send somebody for the law. I'm going to see to it that you're locked up on a charge of attempted murder. Now march, mister!"

McGrath, his lips pressed together in a bloodless line, took a step toward the door. And then halted.

Sutton gestured peremptorily with his gun.

McGrath took another step. And then he bent down

and came up fast with the table in his hands, which he swung as he also swung his body, so that the round Sutton fired at him went wild.

As the table crashed into Sutton, he toppled backward, lost both his balance and his gun, and fell to the floor. As McGrath threw the table at him, Sutton barely managed to roll away in time so that the table hit not him but the wall behind him. He reached for his dropped gun at the same time that McGrath retrieved his. Sutton managed to fire before McGrath could do so, but his shot missed because McGrath had leaped to one side, heading for the window. Before Sutton could fire again, McGrath had scrambled through the window.

Sutton leaped to his feet and ran to the window just in time to see McGrath drop from sight below the overhang. He put one foot through the window, intending to go after McGrath, when he saw the man suddenly reappear. Now McGrath had a woman with him whom he had taken hostage. She was screaming as he held her against him as a shield and dragged her across the street.

Sutton froze. He stood there, half in and half out of the window, and watched helplessly as McGrath fled with the still-screaming woman he had taken prisoner down an intersecting street and out of sight.

Sutton stepped back into his room. He stood there, an image of McGrath's inky eyes and smooth pale face flaring in his mind's eye as he ejected spent shells from his .45 and thumbed cartridges into the cylinder's empty chambers. Then heedless of the fact that his clothes were still damp and he was still tired from his ordeal on the *Mary Malone*, he left his room and headed for the livery stable where he had left his dun upon arriving in San Francisco.

It was late the following day when Sutton first caught sight of the San Joaquin River.

"There's water up ahead," he said in a soft voice to his horse.

The dun's ears twitched and it nickered. It tossed its head and, with no urging from Sutton, moved from a slow walk into a brisk trot.

When horse and rider had reached the western bank of the river, Sutton dismounted and led the dun into a thick stand of willow trees which were crowding each other along the bank. There, he stripped his gear from the animal, and after the horse had drunk its fill, he rubbed it down, using handfuls of short spring grass which, crushed in the process, gave off a sweet smell. After hobbling the dun, he left it to graze the new grass and the moss growing at the base of the willows.

He walked along the riverbank until he came to a spot where cattails grew in profusion. He stopped and, hunkering down on the riverbank, reached out and proceeded to uproot a number of the young twelve-to-eighteen-inch-high plants. His stomach growled as he began to peel off the outer green leaves of each plant, revealing the central core, about six inches long and as white as the inside of a celery stalk. His stomach continued to growl as he began to eat the plants' cores one by savory one, until he had finished them all and his hunger, which had been noisily announced by his stomach, had been appeased.

He remained hunkered down, watching the sun set, listening to the faint whispers of the wind in the willows, glad to be where he was. Cities, he thought. Polite society, he thought. They box a man in and slam the lid down on him. They're too chock-full of pesky rules and regulations that try to tell a man how he can and can't live his own private life.

He blinked as a shaft of sunlight abruptly blazed into bright golden life and then, as the sun sank lower, as abruptly vanished. I should have been born a horse, he thought. One that's never been unlucky enough to know the touch of saddle leather on his back. One that's just lived his life free as wind and water up until the time he's got to do his dying. But me, I keep on bumping into other fellows' rules and regulations until sometimes I just want to up and run and not stop till I can't scent my own kind anymore nor see sign of any other two-legged critter for about a hundred miles around.

He yanked up another cattail, stripped it, and wryly thinking of dessert, ate its core. Then, tossing the plant to the ground, he rose and started back to where he had left his horse. When he reached the spot, he spread his tarp on the ground and then his saddle blanket on top of it beneath one of the willows.

He looked up at the sky and was surprised to see the wispy white clouds which were now scudding across it. As he watched the wind herd the clouds, a saying he had often heard sky-watching and weather-wise farmers recite drifted through his mind.

> Mares' tails and mackerel scales,
> Make lofty ships carry low sails.

Storm coming, he thought, as the mares' tails were transformed by the wind into patchy mackerel clouds. Rain, maybe.

When he heard his dun nickering from within the grove of willows, he tensed. He turned, his hand going for his gun. Now he could see his horse, and he noted the way the animal's ears shot erect, dropped back to lie down along its skull, and then rose to attention again.

He moved fast, heading into the trees at an angle, drawing his .45 as he went, his eyes darting here and there. He saw no one, heard nothing. But someone—or something—was in the woods. That someone or something had been sighted or maybe smelled by his dun, causing the horse to nicker. A deer?

His speculations were interrupted by a sudden whirring that sounded a little like a pheasant leaving its ground cover and taking wing. He turned, stepping to one side as he searched for the precise source of the sound, and his turning saved his life. A hatchet flew past him, uncomfortably close to his head. Its blade tore into a willow behind the spot where he had been standing only a moment ago.

He crouched and headed deeper into the woods after whoever had thrown the hatchet at him, his Colt in his hand, murder on his mind. Trailing his quarry was easy because the sound of someone fleeing through the forest was loud and clear. He increased his pace, ducking low-hanging branches and leaping over deadfalls.

Suddenly, silence.

Sutton halted and stood listening to the silence, wondering where the hatchet thrower had gone. He spotted a slight incline off to his left and moved toward it. He cautiously looked over it, but no one was hiding below the rise. He squinted into the shadow-shrouded trees, which were just beginning to leaf out and which would be thick with full-grown leaves in less than a month. He went back to where he had been standing earlier and then moved forward cautiously, his thumb on the eared-back hammer of his six-gun.

He had gone no more than ten steps when he heard a

whooshing sound behind him. He turned swiftly to find himself facing the Chinese, Ming Long, who, in one fast and fluid motion, knocked the gun from his hand.

Sutton stared at the dagger in Ming Long's hand and then looked up at the broken branch that was dangling just above the head of the Chinese. "You were up in that tree," he said, damning himself for not having detected in time the tactic the man had used to evade him. "What the hell are you doing here?"

When Ming Long spoke, his voice was the confident voice of a thoroughly self-satisfied man. "I am here to kill. You first. Then Kimball when I find him at his cabin here in the mountains."

"How'd you know—" Sutton bit off his words.

"I searched for Ah Toy for a long time but did not find her. So I went to Magdalen House to see if perchance she had returned there. Miss Pritchard told me the girl had not done so when I touched her delicate young throat with this." Ming Long twisted the dagger in his hand and it glinted in the moonlight. "She told me though that Kimball had visited her but swore that she had forgotten to ask him where Ah Toy was.

"And so I asked her where Kimball was, and she told me he had gone into the Sierra Nevada Mountains to a cabin he has on the southern bank of the Stanislaus River. She could not, perhaps because of her fear of me, seem to stop talking. She told me that I would never get to Kimball because you had already gone out after him. That is how I learned that you were also pursuing my prey."

"If you hurt Miss Pritchard—"

Ming Long made a dismissive gesture. "A few small drops of blood from her throat—that cannot be called harming her." He paused momentarily and then said, "I came searching for you to keep you from getting to Kimball first and thus preventing me from finding out from him where he has hidden Ah Toy before I must kill him to avenge my honor, since he has caused me to lose face by helping the girl elude her owner." Ming Long's expression hardened. "Now you—turn around!"

"What's the matter, Ming Long? You afraid to try to take me from the front?" Sutton's eyes dropped to his gun, which lay on the ground. "You'd rather knife an unarmed man in the back, would you?"

"Turn around!" Ming Long shrilled, brandishing the dagger in his hand.

Sutton, his thoughts racing, slowly turned until his back was to Ming Long. He stood without moving a muscle, listening and waiting for Ming Long's expected move. When he heard the Chinese take a step toward him, he threw himself to the ground, somersaulted, sprang to his feet, and spun around. He hurled the dirt and debris he had picked up when he hit the ground into Ming Long's unprotected face.

"*Aieeee!*" the Chinese screamed, dropping his dagger and clawing at his suddenly blinded eyes.

Sutton quickly retrieved his gun. Then, as quickly, he kicked Ming Long's dagger into some underbrush. He was about to pull the trigger of his .45, which was aimed at Ming Long, but he discovered that he could not kill the defenseless Chinese in cold blood. As Ming Long wailed and stumbled blindly about, Sutton struck him on the head with the barrel of his gun.

Ming Long fell to the ground, his cries abruptly silenced, where he lay without moving.

Sutton stood staring down at him for a moment, and then he holstered his Colt, went and got the coil of rope that hung from his saddle horn, and proceeded to bind the unconscious man's hands and feet. After getting his dun ready to ride, he tied his blanket and tarp behind the cantle of his saddle and then boarded the horse and rode away from the spot where he had intended to make camp.

As he rode along the riverbank under a sky in which gray clouds sailed, the trees thinned out and he soon found himself in open country flanked by high hills on both sides of the river. He yawned and continued his journey into and then out of a shallow gorge. The wind rose and lifted his hair and the mane of his horse. He reached up and settled his hat more securely on his head.

He began to whistle as he rode, the melody of *Diamond Joe*. When his dun shied as a piece of shale tumbled down from the ridge above, he began to softly sing the words of the song to quiet the horse.

> I am a pore cowboy, I've got no home;
> I'm here today and tomorrow I'm gone;
> I've got no folks, I'm forced to roam;
> Where I hang my hat is home sweet home.

The dun's ears flickered. It snorted and moved steadily on through the dark night, horse and rider a tall shadow among many others.

> I left my gal in a Texas shack,
> And told her I was a-coming back;

The dun slowed as the ground ahead rose sharply. As Sutton touched his bootheels to the animal's flanks, the horse bobbed its head and began the ascent to higher ground.

> But I lost at cards, then got in jail,
> Then found myself on the Chisholm Trail.

Suddenly, the quiet was shattered by the sound of a rifle shot. Sutton slid out of the saddle as the bullet some-one had fired at him tore into the ground several feet in front of and to the right of his dun. He ran, leading the horse, for the nearest cover—a ragged pile of frost-cracked rubble that had fallen from a rocky outcropping just above it.

As he got down behind it, he put his horse behind him and drew his six-gun. He stared at the trail he had just traveled, wondering who was gunning for him. Some owlhoot sure is, he thought. Nobody's out here hunting. Not in the dark, they're not likely to be. He saw no one. He heard nothing. Ming Long? But the man had no gun that I could see, he thought, only that dagger of his. But he knew that the fact that he'd seen no gun didn't prove that the Chinese hadn't had a gun. It proves only that I didn't see one any more than I saw the horse or wagon that had brought Ming Long into the mountains.

Got to find out who's on my back trail, he thought. Else whoever it is'll keep on stalking me and maybe next time he won't miss. Crouching, Sutton moved to the left, leading his dun, which he then tied to a poplar, leaving the animal sheltered between the tree and the hill behind it. Then, still crouching low, he continued in the direction he had been heading before turning to the right and doubling back along a trail that ran parallel to the one he had been traveling earlier.

From time to time he stopped and listened. Once, he heard the skittering of some unseen creature not far from him and another time the chirping of sparrows he had startled out of sleep. Each time he stopped, he scanned the surrounding countryside, which was composed of rolling slopes, timberland, and small shallow valleys.

It was during one such stop, after he had backtrailed

for nearly a mile, that he thought he spotted movement on the crest of a ridge just ahead and off to the right of his position. He was not really sure he had seen anything, but it had seemed to him that for the briefest of moments someone or something had skylined itself.

He held his position, his eyes on the ridge, his hand gripping his gun, his ears straining to hear any sound that was made by something that was not a natural part of the night.

He stiffened, his eyes and ears still alert, as the sound of twigs snapping reached him. He peered in the direction from which the sound had come—a spot below the ridge where he thought he had seen movement earlier. He could see no one, but the sounds continued. Those are the sounds, he thought, of a man or an animal that's started moving fast. Fast and careless.

But no animal'd trail like that, he thought. What I'm hearing is the sound of somebody bulling their way through the woods over there. Somebody who's headed the way I was headed before I circled back here to where I'm at now. He moved cautiously in the direction of the sounds, which had not diminished, speculating as he went. Whoever it is I'm after's probably the jasper I spotted up on the ridge before. Maybe—

His thoughts dissipated as he caught a faint glimpse of a figure moving in the distance ahead of him. As the figure moved into a small clearing, he saw and recognized the hatless man wearing a broadcloth coat and striped trousers and leading a dapple.

He moved swiftly and silently through the trees, up hummocks and down them, until he was only a few feet from his quarry. "Hold it right there, McGrath!" he ordered. "If you so much as shiver, I'll shoot you!"

Lorne McGrath went rigid. He let go of his dapple's reins and slowly raised his hands. "Who—"

Sutton moved forward, circled the man, and then stood facing him. "Me," he said.

McGrath's eyes widened in disbelief. "But you—you were—" He pointed beyond Sutton.

"I was up there when you took your shot at me. But I doubled back to see if I couldn't find out who was trying to shoot a hole in my hide. I'm not all that surprised to find out it was you."

"Did you find him?"

"Kimball?" When McGrath nodded, Sutton shook his head. "Not yet. But I aim to. I ought to plug you right here and now, McGrath. That looks to me to be the only way to keep you from plaguing me the way you've been doing."

"Don't shoot, Sutton. I'll back off. I will! I'll turn around right now and head back to San Francisco—"

"That's not good enough for me, McGrath. If Kimball should give me the slip and wind up back there, you'll be after him again. I'll bet my bottom dollar on that."

"Then let me go east—back to Virginia City."

Sutton shook his head. "Same problem there, not to mention that should I let you ride east you'll be heading straight toward Kimball's cabin. "Nope, I—"

As Sutton spoke, McGrath took a backward step. Just before Sutton finished speaking, he took another. Then, abruptly lowering both hands, he seized his reins, and jerked hard on them. His dapple screamed as its spade bit tore its flesh and clanked against its teeth. The horse sprang forward and then turned rapidly in a ragged circle. As it did so, its rump struck Sutton broadside, knocking the gun from his hand.

As the horse continued to circle in response to Mc-

Grath's continuing pulls on its reins and bridle, Sutton
leaped out of its way. Then he sprang forward in an
attempt to retrieve his gun, which lay beneath the dapple's wildly twisting and turning body. His fingers were
just about to close on his Colt when McGrath quickly
climbed aboard the dapple and sent his right foot crashing into Sutton's chest.

As Sutton went down, hitting the ground hard, Mc-
Grath drew his Smith & Wesson, took aim, and fired.

His bullet tore up dirt, but, because Sutton had rolled
toward the dapple, preferring to take his chances with
the tormented horse than go up against McGrath and his
gun, he escaped harm. On his knees, he reached out, got a
grip on McGrath's left stirrup, and yanked it. But he
failed to unseat McGrath, who responded with another
vicious kick, this time connecting with Sutton's shoulder.

Sutton hit the ground again. McGrath fired at him
again. Again his round missed Sutton, who sprang to his
feet, his eyes on his gun, which was now on the far side
of McGrath's horse. The dapple reared as its rider, holding too tight a rein on the animal, fought to remain in the
saddle. The horse loomed over Sutton for a split second
and then, as its front hooves started to come down, Sutton scrambled on hands and knees away from the animal.
Then, up and running, he headed for the nearest tree.
When he reached it, he darted behind it and pressed his
body against it as he waited, his chest heaving, to see
what McGrath would do next.

McGrath fired at him, but the bullet hit the tree instead of its intended target. He heeled his horse and
headed for Sutton's refuge, but Sutton had already
turned and was racing away from the tree behind which
he had taken temporary cover. He ran in a broken line

from tree to tree with McGrath galloping after him and quickly shortening the distance between them.

Sutton ran on in a widening circle. Behind him Mc-Grath's progress was slowed by the gradually thickening stand of timber through which Sutton ran as he tried to make his way back to the spot where he had lost his gun.

McGrath let out a roar of rage and kept coming after him. But he was now behind Sutton, who had doubled back as he headed for his destination. When he reached the spot where McGrath had tried to kill him, he dropped down behind the lightning-blasted stump of a sycamore, and as McGrath galloped into sight, he retrieved his .45 and fired at the man. It was a wild shot that caught McGrath in the left shoulder. McGrath let out another roar, which was partly a cry of pain. He veered, evading Sutton, and rode on, heading west.

Sutton turned, raised his six-gun, which he was gripping in both hands, and was about to fire again when McGrath disappeared from sight on the far side of a hummock. Sutton hesitated for only a fraction of a second. Then he turned and raced back to where he had left his dun. He freed the animal, swung into the saddle, and set out in pursuit of McGrath.

But his dun, as it attempted to leap over a half-rotted deadfall that lay across its path, made its move an instant too late. The horse's front hooves struck the deadfall. The animal faltered, lost its balance, and fell heavily to the ground, throwing Sutton out of the saddle.

As the dun went down, Sutton flew through the air and crashed headfirst into the thick trunk of a pin oak. His hat flew from his head and his gun fell from his hand. He lay crumpled at the base of the tree, pain shrieking in his skull, barely aware of the world around him or of his dun, which had gotten to its feet to stand blowing some distance away from him.

Time, for Sutton, seemed to have stopped. Space, for him, had shrunk until it encompassed only the spot where he lay dazed. Fragmented thoughts flickered in his brain. Kimball. McGrath. Got to— His eyes fell on the claw marks high up on the trunk of the tree above him. Grizzly, he thought. It's been staking a claim to this territory. Got to—

He stirred, tried to rise. He wondered what it was he had to do. He slumped back down to the ground, the world around him blurring and whirling crazily. He tried again to get to his feet, and this time he succeeded although he stood swaying like wheat in a big wind. He reached out and held on to the tree for support. This here's the old grizzly's scratch tree, he thought. He blinked several times and then took an unsteady step away from the tree toward the spot where his hat lay on the ground. When he reached it, he bent down slowly, picked it up, and clapped it back on his head. He moved on to where his gun had fallen and picked it up too. He stood there for a long moment with the revolver in his hand, looking about him as if expecting McGrath to reappear at any moment.

His mind began to clear, and he remembered his mission, remembered McGrath, Kimball, the bounty. He whistled through his teeth, but his dun ignored him. He went to where it stood browsing a clump of ragged underbrush and climbed gingerly into the saddle, holding his head at an angle to prevent the pain from returning to it. Now—what? Go after McGrath? No, he decided. He wheeled the dun and moved out at a walk, filling the empty chambers of his six-gun's cylinder as he went, and then holstering it.

The dun was trotting ten minutes later, and Sutton's head was throbbing when he heard a woman's scream. He slammed his heels into the flanks of the dun, which went galloping toward the source of the anguished sound.

Moments later, as he emerged from the trees into a sharply angled clearing, he drew rein, the blood in his veins freezing. He stared, not at Loi Yan, who was crouching in the middle of the clearing with a dagger clutched in her hand, but at a huge grizzly that was snuffling loudly as it padded heavily to and fro in front of Loi Yan, as if it were trying to make up its mind what to do with the creature it had come upon.

Sutton's gun cleared leather. As he aimed it and eared back its hammer, the grizzly spotted him. It stopped snuffling, and a low rumbling noise issued from deep down in its thick throat. As it started shambling toward Sutton, he fired a round at it. He stared in mute alarm as the grizzly kept coming despite the fact that his bullet had plowed into the beast's left shoulder. He was about to fire a second time when the grizzly, as if sensing his intention, suddenly reared up on its hind legs. It let out a roar and its front paws clawed the air.

The dun under Sutton, its great eyes rolling in fear and its breath whistling through its flaring nostrils, backed up. Sutton fought for control of the animal, but it continued backing away from the grizzly that was steadily advancing upon it until its rump struck a tree and it screamed.

Sutton, as the dun's front feet left the ground and it reared wildly, lost his balance and slid out of the saddle. He hit the ground on the left side of the horse and cursed the animal because it moved in front of him, preventing him from getting a second shot at the grizzly.

The bear halted in its tracks as the dun bolted. It stood there for a moment staring down at Sutton, whose vision was blurring, and then its huge head swiveled around and it looked back at Loi Yan, who was now kneeling on the ground, her body rigid, apparently paralyzed by fear.

Sutton steadied himself as he silently begged his vision, which had blurred when he fell, to clear. But it didn't. Before him the figure of the grizzly shimmered, moving slowly in and out of focus. White spots began to fleck its fur, and it took Sutton a moment to realize that the white spots were snowflakes.

The bear, snuffling again, moved in on Sutton, who scrambled to his feet and then slipped and fell down again. As the grizzly came closer to him, Sutton could feel the ground under him shake as the bear's paws struck it like sledgehammers. And then the grizzly attacked. Its right front paw arced downward and Sutton winced as the animal's paw tore through the left sleeve of his buckskin jacket and raked the flesh of his arm.

He fired wildly.

The bear snarled as Sutton's round hit it. It took another savage swipe at Sutton and this time it tore the gun from Sutton's hand. Sutton scrambled backward along the ground as the bear continued to move in on him. He pulled his bowie knife from his right boot and, as the grizzly that was now towering above him was about to drop down on him, he raised the knife he was firmly gripping in his right hand.

Its blade sliced deep into the grizzly's gut. Sutton ripped it upward. He eased backward as the bear's front paws hit the ground and its head hung dazedly down. Sutton plunged his knife into the grizzly's throat. Blood geysered out of the wound, spraying both him and the ground.

The grizzly snuffled, coughed, snuffled again. Its black nose touched the ground. Its legs quivered as Sutton rose and stood warily near it, his bowie dripping blood. A sigh slid through his lips as the grizzly collapsed and rolled over on its side. He sighed again as he saw the bear's eyes begin to glaze. He looked down at the torn sleeve of his jacket, through which he could see the blood on his arm that the grizzly had drawn. He swallowed, and took a deep breath and a final glance at his dead adversary before turning to stare through the thickening snow at Loi Yan, who still knelt motionless on the ground some distance away, her unused dagger still in her hand, her eyes seemingly locked on the carcass of the dead grizzly.

NINE

Sutton bent down and wiped his bowie's blade on some snow-dusted grass before booting it again. Then he picked up his gun and advanced on Loi Yan, who was wearing, over a red bombazine dress, a brown fringed dolman ornamented with black serpentine braid.

As he came up to her, she shuddered and looked up at him. "You are going to kill me."

"Maybe that's what you're fixing to do to me," he countered, his eyes on the dagger in her hand. "Same as the last time you and me met."

Loi Yan shook her head, and her eyes seemed to Sutton to become suddenly sad. She looked off into the distance. "I am a foolish woman. I should not have come alone here to the mountains where bears attack people and snow falls even in the springtime. My buggy—my horse —" She pointed.

Sutton moved away from her, without turning his back on her, to the rim of a deep dry wash. He looked down at the shattered buggy and the bay that was still trapped in its traces and trying feebly to get to its feet. Looking back at Loi Yan, he said, "Your horse, he's busted his left hind leg." He returned his attention to the badly injured animal and then slid down the sloping bank of the wash until he was standing next to the animal which eyed him warily. He bent down toward the bay, placed his gun barrel against the animal's head, and pulled the trigger. The bay's brains and blood spurted out of its destroyed skull to spatter gray and red on the thin coating of snow that was whitening the young spring grass. Sutton turned and climbed up out of the wash. He stood for a moment watching Loi Yan, who was still kneeling, snow flecking her black hair, her face contorted and her shoulders shaking as she wept.

He went to her and held out his hand. Silently, she handed him her dagger, which was, he noted, the same one with which she had tried to stab him in his San Francisco hotel room. He took it from her, thrust it into his waistband, and only then did he holster his Colt.

"You wait right here," he told her.

As he strode away from her, she called out, "Where are you going?" and he heard the fear in her voice that, he supposed, was born of her dread of being abandoned here in the desolate Sierra Nevada during a snowstorm. "Got to round up my horse," he informed her.

It took him some time to locate his dun, but once he had done so, he led it back to where Loi Yan, on her feet now, stood waiting for him. "You're here hunting Kimball," he prodded.

She nodded. "I tried to find Ah Toy in San Francisco, but I couldn't. I went back to Magdalen House, where I had not been since you and I first met. One of the girls there told me that Kimball had been there. She said she heard him tell Miss Pritchard that he was going to a cabin of his here in the mountains that was on the Stanislaus River just this side of the Sonora Pass. She told me that Miss Pritchard, when Kimball had gone, decided to visit you and ask you to try to get him to give himself up. I went at once to a livery, where I rented a horse and buggy, intending to find him before you could, and I— you know the rest."

Sutton's eyes roamed over Loi Yan's body as he searched for any telltale bulge beneath her dolman that would betray the fact that she was concealing a hideout gun or other deadly weapon. He found none. "How come you're risking your neck out here in the mountains for Ah Toy?" he asked her.

"I believe I told you when we first met that Ah Toy is my friend."

"You did. Only most people I've known don't go around trying to kill other folks on behalf of their friends."

"Ah Toy and I are more than merely friends, Mr. Sutton," Loi Yan said with a trace of wistfulness in her voice. "We are more like sisters. We have shared many hardships. I once worked in the house where Ming Long first placed Ah Toy. That was before he sold her to the white man who met her there and desired her for his own. Ah Toy was miserable in that house, as was I. We shared our pain and misfortune. Many times have I held Ah Toy as we both wept the long nights away. Many times have I promised her that life would get better for her—for both of us."

"But it didn't get better for Ah Toy," Sutton remarked. "She went from the house you mentioned to the man Ming Long sold her to."

Loi Yan nodded. "But before she did so, we had become very good friends. We learned—I hope you will not misunderstand what I am about to tell you, Mr. Sutton."

"I'll try hard not to."

"We learned, Ah Toy and I, to love one another very much. She became for me the sister I never had. The child I hope someday to have. I know that if it were I who was missing, Ah Toy would not rest until she had found me. Love, Mr. Sutton, can be a harsh taskmaster. I

hope now you can understand why I tried to keep you
from reaching Mr. Kimball before I did. I had to—have
to find out from him the location of the refuge to which
he took Ah Toy when he first hid her in case she has
returned to it."

Sutton was impressed by what Loi Yan had just told
him but unable to keep from continuing to feel wary
around her.

"Where are you going?" she asked him as he turned
away from her.

"I'm leaving."

"You'll take me with you?" she asked him in a small
uncertain voice.

"I don't want you nowhere near me," he told her
bluntly, "any more'n I'd want to keep close company
with a sidewinder."

"But you can't leave me here," she protested. "I have
no means of transportation. I have no more food. I ate
the last of it hours ago. It's snowing and it's getting dark
— Please, Mr. Sutton. Take me with you."

Sutton hesitated. He wanted to turn and walk away
from Loi Yan. But he knew he couldn't—could but
wouldn't. He was reasonably certain that she would try
to kill him if she got the chance. Well, he thought, resigned to the course of action that seemed to have been
thrust upon him, I won't give the little lady the chance.
I'll keep my eyes and my ears open and the first false
move she makes, I'll—

"Mr. Sutton?"

Instead of answering her, he turned and headed back
toward the spot where the dead grizzly lay sprawled on
the ground. When he reached it, he got down on one
knee and drew his bowie from his boot. As the snow
continued to fall, chilling his exposed hands and face, he

deftly sliced a slab of bloody meat from one of the grizzly's haunches without bothering to skin it first.

He looked back over his shoulder and shouted to Loi
Yan. When he had her attention, he called out, "Bring me
my tarp!"

Moments later she arrived at his side, the tarp in her
hand. He took it from her and spread it out on the
ground. He laid the meat on it and then proceeded to
slice several more slabs from the carcass, which he placed
on the tarp beside the first one.

"What are you doing?" Loi Yan asked him.

"I'm stocking our larder is what I'm doing."

He folded the tarp around the bear meat and then rose.
"We'll make camp for the night over there," he said,
pointing. "Under those poplars. Scout around. See if you
can find some wood for a fire."

"Wood? Where should I look for it?"

"Over there under those trees. Look for a deadfall or
branches that have broken off and fallen down. Haul
what you find over there." Again he pointed to the spot
he had chosen as a campsite.

"Do we have to?" Loi Yan asked him, and when he
gave her a blank look, she added, "Spend the night here, I
mean?"

"You don't have to," he told her. "Not if you don't
want to, you don't."

"Is there someplace civilized near here? A hotel? Some
sort—any sort—of lodging?"

"Nope." He headed for the trees, carrying the tarp
that contained the bear meat. When he reached his dun,
he got a grip on its reins and led the animal in under the
trees, glancing back over his shoulder at the forlorn figure of Loi Yan as she searched in the falling snow for
firewood.

When she returned, he saw the pride on her face as she placed the wood she had gathered in a pile on the ground. She stood there then, looking first at the firewood and then at Sutton.

"That ought to do us," he said, and she smiled at him. He got up and took a small tin container from one of his saddlebags. He took a wooden match from the container, struck it on the heel of his boot, and lit a fire, which was soon burning low but steady. He hunkered down beside the fire and speared one of the slabs of bear meat on a length of green poplar wood. As the meat cooked, he stared into the fire, listening to the rumble of his belly, and licking his lips as some fat fell into the fire, causing a flame to flare up.

Loi Yan stood near him with her arms wrapped protectively around her body.

When the meat was cooked, most of the hair singed from it by the fire, he cut a piece from it, speared it on the end of another piece of green wood, which caused blood to ooze from it, and held it up to Loi Yan. She hesitated a moment and then took it from him. He watched her, wondering at the expression of distaste he saw on her face. And then, as she gingerly bit into the meat and began to chew, he turned back to the fire. He cut himself a piece of the haunch, speared it on the end of his bowie, and began to devour it hungrily.

Sometime later he offered Loi Yan another piece of meat, but she grimaced and refused it. He shrugged his shoulders and proceeded to eat it himself, after which he cooked the remainder of the meat. He stored the meat in his saddlebag, and then, after banking the fire for the night, he offered Loi Yan his ground tarp and blanket.

"It's—it's all bloody," she said with an expression of disgust, indicating the tarp.

"You can put the side that's not next to you."

She shook her head. "I'll take the blanket though, if you don't mind."

He handed it to her and then, carrying his tarp, led his dun to a spot beneath a tall sycamore which was growing just beyond the banked campfire's light, so that neither he nor his horse would be visible to anyone who might come upon the camp during the night. He sat down, his back braced against the trunk of the sycamore, and proceeded to scoop up a handful of snow, which he used to cleanse the wound in his left arm that had been given him by the grizzly. Then, using his bandanna, he bound his torn shirt and jacket in place on his arm, covering the lacerated flesh.

He unholstered his .45 and then wrapped the tarp around his body. He sat there, surreptitiously watching Loi Yan, who was watching him. He smiled to himself when she finally walked off in the opposite direction and, doing as she had seen him do, wrapped his saddle blanket around her and then sat down under a distant tree.

He composed himself for the night, shifting position until he was comfortable and pulling his hat down low on his forehead, almost unmindful of the cold snow that continued to fall. He stared into the fire that was now little more than a soft red glow in the stormy night that had claimed the land. He dozed, snapped awake at the sound of a hunting owl as it flew through the trees above him, and then dozed dreamlessly again.

The faint sound of a horse blowing somewhere in the distance caused him to jerk awake. He sprang to his feet, quickly led his dun deeper into the trees, and automatically glanced up at the sky to determine the time based on the position of the polestar. But the sky was invisible above him because of the snow that was being driven by a strong wind. He peered around the trunk of the poplar where he had taken cover, his hand reaching for his gun, and cursed because of what he saw.

Loi Yan was sitting huddled up close to the fire which was blazing brightly now because she had obviously fed it the rest of the wood that she had gathered earlier.

Sutton, sure that Loi Yan, by building up the fire, had attracted someone to their camp, muttered an oath as he thumbed back the hammer of his Colt and continued squinting into the steadily falling snow. He had been watching the firelit campsite for less than a minute when he saw two mounted figures materialize out of the storm. They rode up to the roaring fire, which was sending up showers of sparks to do fruitless battle with the snow. One of them dismounted and then helped the other one down to the ground.

Sutton could not identify either of the figures because one wore a hat tied down with a scarf and the other's head and shoulders were buried beneath a saddle blanket. He watched as Loi Yan got to her feet and said something to the pair that he could not hear.

Ming Long? And Lorne McGrath? He didn't know, but he intended to try to find out. He cautiously made his way out from behind the poplar and, leaving his dun behind him, eased closer to the trio who were standing close to the fire, his footfalls muffled by the inches-thick carpet of soft snow that now covered the ground. He halted when he could clearly hear their voices, crouching behind the widespread branches of a fir tree.

"But he was right over there!" he heard Loi Yan exclaim. She pointed to the spot where Sutton had intended to spend the night.

"There's no one over there now," the bulkier of the two people said, and Sutton recognized the voice of Marcus Proctor. "He's on his way to get his hands on Kimball, or I miss my guess."

When the person who was wearily leaning against Proctor on his far side turned in the direction Loi Yan had pointed, Sutton found himself staring at the haggard face of Fern Thorndyke. He listened as Loi Yan hurriedly explained to Proctor and Fern who she was and what she was doing there. As he continued listening to the conversation taking place among the three people, his expression grew grim.

"We also want to keep Sutton from getting to Kimball," Proctor told Loi Yan earnestly. "We ran into him at a stage stop back along the trail where Miss Thorndyke—"

"I arranged with a man named Carter, who was on the stage with us, to kill Sutton," Fern interrupted, her voice faint.

"Carter failed in his mission," Proctor stated morosely, "although the next day he assured us he had successfully completed the task for which Miss Thorndyke paid him quite handsomely."

"Mr. Sutton, it seems, may well have as many—perhaps more—lives than the proverbial cat," Fern said. "Mr. Proctor, in a noble effort to protect me from Mr. Sutton, hired a man named Bad Ed Kelvin in Virginia City to do away with our nemesis. But Kelvin, like Carter, failed to do so."

"But how did you know that Sutton was here?" Loi Yan asked.

It was Fern who answered her. "I received a letter from Mr. Kimball telling me to join him in San Francisco as soon as possible. I came here with Mr. Proctor, who insisted upon accompanying me since he was worried that Sutton might harm me to keep me from warning Mr. Kimball about him.

"When we reached San Francisco and discovered that Mr. Kimball had dropped out of sight, I made periodic visits both to his boardinghouse and to his office building in the hope that he would turn up at one or perhaps both places."

"He didn't," Proctor volunteered, "for the obvious reason that the police were waiting for him in both places. But on one of our visits to his office building, the janitor told us that a man answering Sutton's description had been at the building asking about Mr. Kimball."

"But the old fool couldn't recall the name of the hotel at which Sutton had told him he was staying," Fern interjected angrily.

"Not until two days ago did he recall the name of the hotel," Proctor stated almost as angrily. "Miss Thorndyke and I then took turns watching Sutton's hotel and his movements. When I saw him go to the livery and then leave town, I was certain that he had discovered Kimball's whereabouts, so Miss Thorndyke and I followed him."

"But we lost track of him in the snow a while back," Fern declared. "We kept searching for him and then we saw your fire—"

"We thought it might be his—that we'd found him at last," Proctor interrupted.

"He was here!" Loi Yan insisted, looking around her.

"We spied on your camp for some time before we rode in," Proctor continued. "But we saw no sign of him. Sutton has undoubtedly abandoned you, my dear, and gone off on his own again after Mr. Kimball."

"We'll go after him," Fern declared firmly.

"Unarmed?" Loi Yan asked fearfully.

"We are not unarmed, my dear," Proctor assured her as he drew a four-shot Colt Cloverleaf house pistol from a shoulder holster and displayed it to Loi Yan.

Fern smiled and withdrew from her pocket a petite Remington Elliot .22 for Loi Yan to see before pocketing it again.

Sutton eased away from the fir tree and moved deeper into the woods until he reached his dun. He swung into the saddle, turned the horse—and found himself facing what for a startled instant he took to be an apparition standing in his path.

"As you can see, I managed to free myself," Ming Long stated tonelessly, and raised his hand to hurl at Sutton the dagger it held.

Sutton's .45 cleared leather. He fired.

Ming Long was lifted off the ground and thrown backward against a tree, his arms flailing. He stared balefully at Sutton. He blinked and tried to throw the dagger in his hand. But it slipped from his fingers as he slid down along the length of the tree and then fell face forward in the snow.

Sutton slammed his heels into his horse and went galloping away, leaving behind him the campsite and the bonfire Loi Yan had built, which was dying down now as the still-falling snow fought to smother it.

They're all pretty much greenhorns when it comes to trailing, he thought as he rode on through the white night. But they've had themselves some beginner's luck when it comes to running me down. But I could have wiped out all three of them at the camp back there the same as I did Ming Long. A grim image of the Chinese lying sprawled in the snow ghosted across his mind. I've still got four to watch out for, he thought. Loi Yan. Fern Thorndyke. Lorne McGrath. Marcus Proctor. No, five.

There's Ted Kimball too, he reminded himself. And Kimball, from what I've heard tell about his murdering ways, won't go down easy. So it's five against one. Not the best odds in the world. But I've been up against worse in my time.

He rode on, keeping his head down in a largely futile effort to keep the sleet that had joined the snow from stinging his face. The tactic was only partially successful however. The sleet seemed to seek out his exposed skin, pelting it sharply and finding its way beneath the up-turned collar of his buckskin jacket.

Around him the night seemed deceptively bright be-cause of the snow, but it was, in grim reality, crow black. Sutton could see no more than two feet—and at times only a foot or less—in front of him. His feet were cold and his bare hands, which he blew on from time to time, felt frozen. His dun swayed as it plowed through the thickening drifts, threatening at times to pitch him from the saddle. But he remained aboard his mount, letting it pick its own slow pace over the mountainous terrain that was sprinkled with fir trees which stood like stout white sentinels with their long-needled arms outstretched to bar any intruder's passage.

Except for the occasional whine of the wind as it keened its way down into mountain valleys and up along sharp slopes, the night was silent. Sutton had an eerie sense of being in a world that was not quite real, one suspended somewhere in another realm, where snow ruled with a cold cruel hand that could, he knew, uncar-ingly kill.

He had heard tales told by drovers of snowstorms in which cattle, as snow melted on their warm bodies and then refroze to form icicles, had lost patches of their hides as the icicles grew heavy and broke away. He had heard tales told of cattle breathing in so much sleet that they suffocated.

Hours later his dun came to a sudden halt and stood with its head hanging down, not moving a muscle. Sutton dismounted, suspecting what was wrong, and when an investigation confirmed his suspicions, he proceeded to cup his hands around the horse's eyes, one after the other, and blow on them to thaw the frozen snow that had blinded the animal.

From his saddlebags he took his extra sheepskin-lined cinch, which he wrapped around the lower part of his face. He also removed a pair of socks which he pulled over his hands to serve him as makeshift gloves. Then, getting a grip on the reins, he began to lead the dun through the storm, picking his way carefully but, despite his caution, occasionally sinking into hip-high drifts.

He kept his head down and his free hand thrust into a pocket of his jeans. From time to time as he covered one slow mile after another, he switched hands, but the numbing cold stole so much feeling from his exposed sock-covered hand that he could barely feel the reins he was gripping. Recognizing the numbness in his hands for the warning that it was, he halted and stripped off the socks he had put on a short time ago. He bent down and scooped up some snow that was only a little whiter than the flesh of his frostbitten fingers. He rubbed it vigorously on his fingers, and he kept scooping up more snow and rubbing it on his fingers until at last most of the dead whiteness left his flesh and the blood began to flow once again.

He tossed away his pair of snow-soaked socks and moved on, alternately thrusting his right and then his left hand into his pocket, the sleet stinging his face and his legs becoming leaden. When the dun nickered, he turned back to the horse and looked down as the animal lowered its head and nipped at its own front legs, which had been, he saw with dismay, cut in places by the thin crust of ice that had formed on the surface of the fallen snow.

He spoke to the animal, called it brave, told it that it had a heart as big as a barn, urged it on. The dun responded to his words and to the surprisingly gentle touch of his hard hand on its neck. It moved gallantly on when Sutton did, its head hanging down but its gait steady.

Sutton didn't know exactly how many miles he had traveled when his legs suddenly gave way under him and he went down. The dun nickered and stood over him, looking down at him and blinking its liquid eyes. Sutton gripped his right boot in which his foot felt like an insensate club. So, he soon discovered, did his left one.

Frostbite, he knew, was the reason he had no feeling in either foot.

He pulled hard on his left boot but was not, for a long time, able to remove it because he could not move his foot. But finally he managed to yank it off.

He stripped off his sock and began to massage his foot with snow as vigorously as he could, fighting against the urge to sleep that was welling up within him and that he knew was the snow's cold lure which, if heeded, would lead him to an icy death. For a long time he could feel not the slightest sensation in his foot, but then, at last, when he had almost begun to despair, searing pain stabbed through his toes as he managed to curl them slightly. He pulled on his sock and then his boot and repeated the process with his other foot. He welcomed the pain that was piercing his toes and feet because he knew that the pain meant life.

He got to his feet and stood there unsteadily for a moment as wave after wave of weariness washed over him. He shook his head to clear it. He deliberately bit his lower lip, but the pain he caused himself did not drive away the almost overpowering urge he had been feeling over the course of the last several miles to simply drop in his tracks, curl up in the snow that had begun to seem so inviting to him, and surrender to the blissful sleep which would blot out the bitterly cold world surrounding him.

But he kept stubbornly on, putting one determined foot in front of the other and keeping his head down in the storm that was steadily increasing in intensity. The rising wind howled its way down from the summits of the mountains, turning what had been a simple snowstorm into a full-fledged blizzard. Trees bent toward the ground beneath the onslaught of the whistling wind, and some of their branches broke and fell to the ground under the snow's wet weight.

Twice Sutton's dun went down. Once it foundered for several minutes in a deep drift into which it had stumbled as it pulled to one side of Sutton in an attempt to escape the wind that tore down through a gully toward it. Another time it simply dropped, its muzzle half-buried in the snow, its ears laid back along its head. Both times Sutton had to coax and goad and coax again to get the animal back on its feet and moving once more into the punishing wind.

When he came to a tributary of the Stanislaus River which ambled at a right angle across his path, he almost gave up. The water was too deep to ford, which meant that if he was to continue heading north in the direction of the Sonora Pass, he would have to turn east temporarily in order to circle around the tributary at the point where it finally ended. And where, he wondered dismally, did it end? How many miles from where he now was did it end? He considered taking shelter somewhere. But where? he asked himself with little hope as he looked around at the crystalline landscape. He saw no suitable place and knew that even if he could find some sort of satisfactory cover, he would be endangering both his dun and himself by stopping out in the open. Remaining for long in one spot without moving would mean, he knew, that he and his horse might very well freeze to death.

He drew a deep breath, let it out, and walked doggedly on despite his severely cramped muscles, the river's tributary on his left. He almost missed the spot where it ended. He had been walking with his eyes slitted, conscious only of the snow and the biting cold and the mournful voice of the wailing wind, when he suddenly realized that there was no longer any sign of water on his left. He turned and started back and was at last once again traveling north toward the Sonora Pass with the Stanislaus' tributary behind him.

Hours later, he saw what he thought at first was an illusion. Ahead of him in the distance a light glowed golden. He halted and closed his eyes. He opened them again. The light was still there like a small beacon beckoning to him. Without quite realizing what he was doing, he stretched out a hand as if reaching for the light. He made a guttural sound deep in his throat as his outstretched hand blocked the light. And then, realizing why the light had vanished, he lowered his hand and started moving toward it, forcing his exhausted body to keep moving.

As he came closer to the light, still leading his slow-moving dun that he feared might be dying on him, he realized that it was not a fire. The light was coming through the window of a cabin. A cabin, he thought. A cabin on the southern bank of the Stanislaus River. *Kimball's cabin?*

It had to be! But was it really?

He plowed gamely on through several snowbanks, having to lift each foot high into the air before putting it down again, his eyes on his destination—the cabin's door that was faintly visible now next to its lamplit window.

He had almost reached it when his legs gave out on him and he fell. He was up on his knees almost instantly, but snow avalanched down upon him from where it was piled halfway up the cabin door. He clawed his way through it with his free hand, holding tightly to the dun's reins with his other hand. He crawled the last few feet to his destination, shivering violently, and when he reached the door, he tried the doorknob but found the door locked. He pounded on it, waited a moment, then when he received no response, continued pounding on it. Cursing incoherently, he staggered upright and kicked the door.

When it remained closed, he sagged against it, half-standing and half-sitting in the cold snow, his head resting against its rough boards, too weak now to do anything more.

And then he heard the music. The music of a fiddle. It lilted and it flowed from beyond the door where the world was warm and safe and he tried to shout "Kimball!" But no name emerged from his throat. He raised his arm and struck the door with his fist. Once. Twice.

The music abruptly stopped.

He tried again to shout Kimball's name, but no sound came from his mouth.

The door opened.

Yellow lamplight spilled from the cabin to stain the pristine snow outside.

Sutton tried to raise his head but couldn't. "My horse," he said, the words merely a whisper. "He's freezing to—to—" He couldn't say the word "death," didn't want to say it. His lips closed and he fell unconscious across the cabin's doorsill.

TEN

The devil fiddled and they all danced.

Fern Thorndyke. Marcus Proctor. Loi Yan. Lorne Mc-Grath. And even Ming Long, gaily risen from the dead, pranced hand in hand with Fern in a merry circle while all the others danced with smiles on their faces and murder in their hearts.

Sutton tried to escape from their midst, but the devil prodded him with his fiddler's bow and Sutton was forced to dance now with Fern and then with Loi Yan, who tried again to kill him.

The music reached a crescendo. The dancers, all but Sutton, joined hands, and as they advanced on him in a gory gavotte that was characterized by thunderous gunfire and knives and hatchets slicing like screams through the air, he turned and fled from them.

The devil howled like the wind and fiddled even faster.

Sutton ran and ran, the infernal music and the would-be murderers pursuing him relentlessly until he reached an all-white world that had a heart of ice and no safe place for him in it anywhere.

The music turned melancholy, morbid, as they all came stalking Sutton, one by dangerous one. Fern with a sharp icicle in her hand. Proctor with glittering hoarfrost where his eyes had been. McGrath moving as fast and as invisibly as the wind. Loi Yan with snowflakes in her black hair and mayhem in her eyes.

He cried out to them, told them that he didn't want to kill them. They kept coming. The gun in his hand spat first lead and then fire, but it did so too late because they had all fallen upon him and they were dragging him down. He fought them—fought them as hard as he could with both hands and with both feet, with his teeth . . .

Breathlessly, he gasped his way back into consciousness, and the music that had invaded his deadly dream played on and he realized that it was real. He tried to rise from the rope bed on which he discovered he was lying, but he fell helplessly back upon it.

The music stopped.

A moment later he was staring silently up at a familiar face. "How come you took me in, Kimball?" he asked. "How come you just didn't let me lay out there and freeze to death when you saw who it was had come calling on you?"

"I wouldn't—couldn't do that," Kimball answered dully. Then with a wan smile: "I must admit though that I rather hoped my violin music might do you in." He placed his violin and bow on a nearby table.

Sutton's eyes roamed about the rude cabin. He noted his cartridge belt and buckskin jacket, which were draped over the back of a chair on the seat of which sat his hat and below which were his boots. His eyes returned to his holstered .45.

"I'm not going to try to shoot you, Sutton," Kimball volunteered. "Surely you realize that if I had wanted to kill you, I could have done so while you slept."

"How long have I been here?"

"A day and a half. You slept straight through without waking up once."

"My horse?"

"It's with my roan in a three-sided shed I've got out

back. The shed faces south, so it's fairly snug. I watered
and grained both horses this morning. The storm's all
over. They both came through it pretty well." Kimball
paused. "How did you find me?" he asked then in a voice
that suddenly sounded both weary and woebegone.

"It wasn't easy," Sutton replied, and proceeded to pro-
vide a lengthy answer to Kimball's question.

"You mean to say that Fern and Marcus Proctor are on
their way here? That they paid two men to kill you? I
don't believe it."

"Believe it, Kimball, on account of it's the truth I told
you."

"And the woman who says she's a friend of Ah Toy's—
you said her name is—"

"Loi Yan."

"She's also trying to find me in order to learn the
whereabouts of Ah Toy? And you claim she too tried to
kill you?"

"She was afraid if I got my hands on you before she
could talk to you, you might wind up dead and she might
never find out where Ah Toy is—if you know where she
is. Ming Long—he was after you for helping Ah Toy get
away from the man he sold her to, and he was after me to
keep me from maybe having to kill you before he could.
McGrath—well, he just wants revenge on you for killing
his brother, and he doesn't want me standing in the way
of him getting that revenge."

Kimball sighed. He ran his fingers through his hair.
"Fern and I were planning to run away together. I wrote
to her in Virginia City. We were to meet in San Francisco. But then the police must have been notified about
me by the authorities in Virginia City. They staked out
my office and my boardinghouse so that I never did have

an opportunity to meet Fern as we'd planned before I left Virginia City following the murder."

"Why'd you kill McGrath?" Sutton asked.

"What?" Kimball stared at Sutton, a frown on his face. "Oh—yes, why did I—McGrath was assaulting Fern when I entered his office. He was trying to—" Kimball lowered his head. Then, looking up at Sutton again: "And you say Lorne McGrath is trying to find me so that he can kill me."

"Lorne McGrath's out to kill you all right, Kimball, but I'm not. Not unless you force me to, I'm not."

"Well, if I get back to Virginia City alive—if McGrath doesn't outwit you, Sutton, and do me in, I'll at least be able to hire myself a high-priced lawyer."

"From all I'd heard while I was hunting you, you're down on your luck, Kimball. You couldn't keep on paying Lady Dora for the use of that hellhole she let you use in Chinatown, but here you are now talking about hiring a pricey counselor-at-law. That's a pretty good trick if you can pull it off."

"No trick. A simple matter of economics. Before I left Virginia City for good following the murder of McGrath, I turned over a thousand shares of badly depressed stock I owned in the Comstock Lode's Silver Queen Mine to my longtime friend Marcus Proctor, with orders for him to sell it if and when the shares ever reached the price at which I had originally purchased them.

"I learned after I fled from San Francisco that the stock has recently soared to a bid price of nearly two hundred dollars per share—shares I had originally bought at forty dollars each." Kimball shrugged philosophically. "If I had held on to my shares instead of ordering Marcus to sell them when and if they reached forty dollars a share, I would now have not merely forty thousand dollars but two hundred thousand dollars, less Marcus' commission in both cases, of course. Well"—Kimball shrugged again —"that sad matter is water over the dam now, and I shall be content with the not inconsiderable sum of forty thousand dollars that Marcus has realized for me."

Sutton rose and made his way to the cabin's window. He looked up at the sun, which had just passed its meridian in the cloudless sky. "We'd best be on our way, Kimball."

"On our way where?"

"I'm taking you back to Virginia City with me, where you'll stand trial for the murder of Dade McGrath," Sutton replied as he went to the chair next to the bed, sat down in it, and proceeded to pull on his boots. He was up on his feet and drawing his gun the instant Kimball turned sharply away from him. "Where do you think you're going, Kimball?"

Kimball turned back, an innocent expression on his face. "My coat—I've got to get it. It's still unusually cold outside for this time of year. Do you mind?"

"Get it." Sutton holstered his gun and strapped his cartridge belt around his hips. He slipped into his buckskin jacket as Kimball put on and buttoned up his coat.

When Kimball turned back toward him, Sutton gestured with his gun and Kimball started for the door. So did Sutton.

Kimball was halfway to it when he suddenly lunged toward the wooden table that separated him from Sutton, upended it and picked up a wooden chair. Sutton threw up his right arm to protect his head and face as Kimball brought the chair crashing down upon him.

He took the brunt of the blow on his shoulder, but one of the legs of the chair cracked against his ribs, sending slivers of pain slicing through him. He tried to get to his feet, but as he did so, the room began to spin. He supported himself with his hands pressed against the floor, his head hanging down, and his vision rapidly darkening. My gun, he thought, as his shoulders began to throb painfully and his ribs began to feel as if one or more of them had been broken. As his fingers closed on his holstered gun's grips, he lost consciousness.

When he looked up an unknown amount of time later, Kimball was gone. The cabin door was open and swaying back and forth in the almost balmy spring breeze that was making its way into the cabin. He struggled to his feet and almost fell over the chair that Kimball had so successfully used as a club on him. He made his way to the open door, where he blinked and then shut his eyes against the blinding glare of sun on snow.

His eyes snapped open when he heard a horse nicker nearby. A moment later Kimball, mounted on a roan, rode around the southern side of the cabin.

Sutton was about to fire a round at the fleeing man, but something stopped him from doing so. Instead, he raced after Kimball. When he was close enough to him, he vaulted up over the rump of the roan and knocked Kimball out of the saddle. As Kimball hit the ground and the breath whooshed out of his lungs, Sutton leaped from the saddle and hauled Kimball to his feet. He drew back his right arm and threw a haymaker that slammed into Kimball's unprotected jaw. As Kimball went down, Sutton reached for him again, and again he hauled the hapless man to his feet. This time he delivered a powerful right cross and followed it up with a pair of savage left jabs that left Kimball bent over and barely able to breathe.

Sutton let go of the man and stepped back. He gave a grunt of satisfaction as Kimball's knees buckled and he went down. "Get up!" he ordered, and when Kimball had struggled to his feet, where he stood wiping the blood from a gash Sutton had opened on his jaw, Sutton added, "Go get your horse."

When Kimball had done so, he muttered, "I should have shot you to death back in the cabin when you were unconscious and I had the chance."

"Why the hell didn't you?" Sutton asked, wondering why Kimball had chosen instead to flee.

Kimball turned away from him without answering the question.

"Let's ride," Sutton muttered, and Kimball, without giving him so much as another glance, climbed into the saddle of the roan.

Sutton drew his gun, made sure that Kimball saw it, and said, "I aim to collect the bounty money offered for you, Kimball, and I'll do whatever it takes to make sure I do collect it. Which includes killing you if you make one false move. You got that, have you?"

Kimball didn't answer the question.

Sutton shrugged. "Move out."

As Kimball obeyed the order, Sutton yelled, "Not that way! We're heading east. You've seen the last of San Francisco for a while."

Kimball wheeled his roan and rode east with Sutton trailing right behind him, his gun still in his hand.

They had gone less than a mile when from behind them came a loud shout. Sutton looked back over his shoulder to find riders moving swiftly toward him and Kimball. A moment later Kimball exclaimed, "It's Fern! It's Fern and Marcus and—is that the woman named Loi Yan you told me about who is mounted behind Marcus?"

"That's her," Sutton said, and drew rein. He sat his

saddle, Colt in hand, and waited until the trio had ridden up to join him and Kimball.

"Oh, Ted!" Fern cried as she dismounted and ran to Kimball, who slid out of his saddle and took her in his arms. "Oh, it's so wonderful to see you at last. Are you all right? Let me look at you!" She held him at arm's length. "You've lost weight." Then she took him in her arms again, kissing his face and hugging him hard.

"I see you succeeded in apprehending your quarry, Mr. Sutton," Proctor commented as he and Loi Yan dismounted. "And without harming him. Perhaps Miss Thorndyke and I—and Loi Yan as well—perhaps we all were unduly apprehensive about the mores and manners of a bounty hunter. On the other hand, you did kill the man Loi Yan told us was named Ming Long back at your campsite."

Sutton stared wordlessly at Proctor's now badly misshapen face, the result, he knew, of a bad case of hives caused by the cold. Proctor's eyes were nearly swollen shut, their lids and lashes crusted with mucus. Because his nostrils were also nearly swollen shut, his breath came in gusty bursts through his puffy lips.

Sutton shifted his gaze to Loi Yan, noting that the tip of her nose was the color of ashes and there were similar grayish spots on her ears. Frostbite, he thought.

"No, really, Fern," Kimball was saying, "I'm quite all right. Sutton didn't harm me, and I'm sure he really doesn't want to—but never mind about me. What about you? Are you all right? You really shouldn't have come after me. You might have been hurt or—"

Fern put a finger on Kimball's lips to silence him. Then she kissed him again and rested her left cheek against his chest.

"I beg your pardon, Mr. Kimball," Loi Yan said tentatively as he gazed at her over Fern's head. "I—"

"You want to know the whereabouts of Ah Toy," Kimball interrupted. "Well, I shall be happy to tell you what you want to know. When I first found Ah Toy after she had escaped from the man to whom Ming Long sold her, I took her to the apartment of the woman who worked as my secretary in my law office in San Francisco. That was before I knew about Miss Roberta Pritchard's Magdalen House and about the wonderful work she does there.

"Well, just before I was forced to leave San Francisco, I paid a visit to my secretary and discovered to my surprise that Ah Toy had returned to her. We all agreed that Ah Toy should remain with my secretary until such time as it was deemed safe to turn her over once again to the kindly hands and kindlier heart of Miss Pritchard. Ah Toy may still be with my secretary, but if she is not, she is undoubtedly once again with Miss Pritchard."

"Thank you very much, Mr. Kimball," Loi Yan murmured when he had given her the address of his secretary in San Francisco. "I shall return at once and seek out my good friend."

"Ted," Fern said, stepping away from him. "If only I'd known that your secretary knew of your whereabouts, I could have contacted her and—"

"She didn't know, my dear," Kimball said. "I simply told her that I was leaving town and that I wanted to wish her well before I left."

Kimball turned to Proctor. "Marcus, I was telling Mr. Sutton that I learned that my shares in the Silver Queen Mine, which I asked you to sell for me at forty dollars per share, are now worth two hundred dollars per share. Would that I had waited."

"Ah, Ted, my boy," Proctor declared, his words

blurred as they emerged from his swollen lips. "I have great good news for you. You still own your thousand shares of stock in the Silver Queen."

"I still own—"

"You'll recall that you stored your stock certificates in your personal strongbox, which you then left with me."

"Yes, I did, but, Marcus, I'm afraid I don't understand—"

"Ted, dear boy, you gave me the strongbox but you failed to give me the key to it, an oversight I did not become aware of until after you had vanished and the stock began to rise in price."

Kimball's hand went to his vest pocket, from which he drew a gold watch. He held it up, smiling broadly. He shook it, and the tiny key that dangled from the watch chain glittered in the sunlight. "The key to my strongbox," he announced.

"You are a very rich man now, Ted," Proctor exclaimed, his eyes glittering like Kimball's key, at which he was avidly staring. "Sell your shares in the Silver Queen now and—well, as I said, you may not be quite as rich as Croesus, but you run that estimable gentleman a respectable second, I do declare!"

Fern stared forlornly at Kimball. "But this marvelous good fortune comes so hard upon the heels of an even greater misfortune." She turned and glared at Sutton.

"I reckon," he said mildly, "it's time to be moseying on. Mount up, Kimball."

When Kimball hesitated, Sutton raised the barrel of his gun slightly so that it was aiming at Kimball's throat. Kimball, blanching nearly as white as the snow beneath his feet, climbed quickly into the saddle.

"Move out," Sutton ordered as he kept his eyes on the two women and one man who were all dividing their attention between him and Kimball, who had turned his horse and was riding east.

Sutton followed him, riding at an angle so that he could keep in sight the trio of people who were watching his departure without losing sight of Kimball.

He saw Fern take an uncertain step toward him, and he noticed the way Proctor's head was swiveling as the man scanned the trees that grew off to the south under a ridge. Those three sure do look skittish to me, he thought uneasily. Like as if they're maybe about to make some kind of a move on me.

"Don't you folks try anything," he warned them at the top of his voice. "You do and I'll take some of you down with me."

But when the shot he had been expecting came, it came, to Sutton's surprise, not from either Fern or Proctor but from the trees behind him.

He wheeled his dun and was about to fire at whoever had fired at him, but he saw no one. Not at first. But then, as Fern, in the distance, screamed, "Kill him!" he saw the gunman emerge from the trees. He got off a snap shot that came close but not close enough to Lorne Mc-Grath, who stood crouching in the snow, his Smith & Wesson .44 tightly clutched in both of his hands.

Sutton realized that McGrath was not aiming at him but at Kimball, who was still aboard his horse, which was circling nervously because Kimball had too tight a grip on its reins. He fired, but he was too late. McGrath had dived for cover behind the snowy trunk of the nearest tree. "Take cover!" he yelled to Kimball, but again he was too late, because Kimball's horse reared, throwing its rider into a snowdrift. Sutton was just about to slam his bootheels into his dun's flanks and go after McGrath, who was clearly trying, now that he had caught up with his quarry, to kill Kimball.

But then Proctor's Colt Cloverleaf suddenly appeared in his hands and he aimed it, to Sutton's absolute amazement that quickly became utter disbelief, at Kimball, who was emerging from the snowdrift into which he had fallen.

"Down, Kimball!" Sutton shouted, and when Kimball merely stood there and dazedly gazed around him, he galloped toward Proctor, firing a warning round over the man's head as he went. But his shot went unheeded by Proctor, who was in the saddle and galloping toward Kimball.

Sutton veered and cut Proctor off. He lashed out at the man, and the barrel of his Colt struck Proctor on the right temple, unhorsing the man and sending him down into the snow.

"Kill him!" Fern screamed again, her voice shrill and sounding demented as she plowed clumsily through the snow, heading toward Kimball.

Proctor struggled up out of the snow, his Cloverleaf still in his hand. Sutton leaned over and struck him again with his gun. This time Proctor fell unconscious to the ground. Sutton headed for Fern, but his dun stumbled into a deep rut that had been hidden by the snow, almost throwing him. But he remained in the saddle, and as Fern suddenly stopped only two feet away from Kimball and raised the Remington .22 she had taken from her pocket, Sutton yelled *"Kimball!"* at the top of his voice.

The man seemed to awaken from a dream—or a nightmare. He shook his head. He held out a defensive hand toward Fern.

"Get down, dammit!" Sutton yelled at him as he managed to get his dun up and out of the snowy rut into

which the animal had stumbled. To his relief, Kimball dropped down behind a snowbank and was lost from sight. Sutton urged his horse on, but it moved slowly despite his tugging on the reins, obviously afraid of falling again, clearly wary of the unseen terrain beneath its hooves.

Sutton groaned as he saw McGrath come running out of the trees toward the spot where Kimball had just vanished in the snow. He fired a round at McGrath and was gratified to see the man spin around and away from him as a result of the bullet's impact. He headed toward Fern, who was searching in vain for Kimball, cursing his dun for moving much too slowly to suit him. He didn't understand what was happening. But he did understand that they were all—all of them except Loi Yan, who stood as still as any statue—determined to kill, not him, but Ted Kimball. It makes no sense, he thought, as ahead of him the snow stirred and Kimball's head and shoulders emerged from it.

Fern emptied her gun at Kimball.

Kimball cried out in pain, and Sutton saw blood from the man's left forearm redden the white snow.

He rode on and managed to place himself between Kimball and McGrath who was now sprinting toward Kimball. *"Hold it, McGrath!"* he yelled. *"Don't move or you're dead!"*

McGrath, blinking in the blinding glare caused by the sunlight that was being reflected from the snow's surface, halted, hesitated, and then took another step toward Kimball.

Sutton aimed a round over his head.

McGrath dropped his gun, which vanished in the snow. He raised his hands.

But Sutton had only the slightest taste of victory, because at that moment he became aware, out of the corner of his eye, of Proctor rising to his feet from the snow like a malevolent apparition and taking aim again at Kimball.

"Don't do it, Proctor!" Sutton shouted. "Don't—"

But Proctor did. He fired three rounds in quick succession, all of which missed Kimball, and he was about to fire a fourth when Sutton moved his dun forward and placed it and himself between Proctor and Loi Yan on the one side and Kimball, Fern, and McGrath on the other.

Proctor ran clumsily through the snow in an attempt to get a better shot at Kimball, but before he could fire again, Sutton did.

Proctor dropped. Fern cried out and ran to where he lay sprawled, limbs akimbo, in the bloody snow.

She looked up at Sutton and shrieked, "He's dead! You've killed him!"

Sutton turned his attention to McGrath, who had retrieved his gun from the snow where it had fallen. "I'll do the same for you, mister," he told McGrath, "if you don't drop that gun."

McGrath swore. He dropped the gun. He raised his hands.

"Now, will somebody tell me just what the hell's going on here?" Sutton bellowed.

No one answered him. Fern angrily tossed her empty gun away. Loi Yan sank to the snow, where she sat with her arms wrapped around her body, her eyes closed. McGrath stood with compressed lips, his hands held high above his head, glaring balefully at Kimball, who was staring intently at Fern, his wounded left arm dangling at his side. Proctor lay motionless on the ground, staring sightlessly up at the sun.

"Why, Fern?" Kimball murmured. "Why did you try

to kill me? You and Marcus both? I can understand why
McGrath tried to gun me down but—Fern, why?"

She looked up and then away at nothing. In a lifeless
voice she replied, "Someday you might have told the
truth, Ted."

The truth about what, Sutton wondered as his eyes
darted from her to Kimball and then back again.

"Never!" Kimball insisted. "Fern, I promised you I
wouldn't. It was all my idea to do what I did and say
what I said. You didn't want me to do it. You wanted to
tell the truth about what happened. At least at first you
did."

"Marcus—" Fern turned back to confront Kimball.
"He was one of my lovers."

"Marcus was one of your—" Kimball began in a
stricken voice but couldn't continue.

"Dade McGrath was another."

Kimball began to shake his head slowly from side to
side.

"Dade was becoming a bore," Fern continued. "He
wanted me to marry him, but I wouldn't. He had taken
to pleading with me. He became weak. Disgusting. Not a
real man at all."

"But, Fern, you said you loved me," Kimball protested,
still shaking his head. "We were going to be married."

"I never loved you, Ted Kimball. I used you for my
own pleasure. You were young, unlike Dade McGrath
and Marcus Proctor. You had promised to take me to San
Francisco where I just knew I would, once I got there,
find a way to conquer the city—the whole world. But
then—things suddenly changed."

Fern brushed back a strand of her hair that had fallen
across her forehead before continuing. "It was noble of
you, Ted, to do what you did for me. And everyone be-

lieved the story you told, even Marcus did. Later, when he mentioned to me the stock in the Silver Queen Mine that you left with him to sell for you, I convinced him that he had to try to kill you. I pointed out to him that once you were dead, no one would be the wiser about the money he had gained from the sale of your stock, so he and I could share it.

"So you see, Ted, Marcus had a very good reason for trying to kill you. I had an even better one. I was afraid that one day you might tire of me and decide to tell the truth about what actually happened that day in Dade McGrath's office.

"But then he"—Fern turned and pointed a trembling finger at Sutton—"came upon the scene and everything began to go wrong."

Suddenly, Sutton was certain that he knew what Fern was talking about. "It wasn't Ted Kimball who brained Dade McGrath with that poker, was it, Miss Thorndyke? It was you who killed him, wasn't it?"

"*Yes!* He was pawing me and slobbering all over me and crying and begging me not to leave him when Ted came into the office and saw me hit and kill Dade with the poker. I was tired of Dade, but he couldn't—or wouldn't—understand that. He thought we were going to be together *forever.*" Fern began to giggle hysterically.

McGrath let out a roar of rage, made a grab for his dropped gun, and came up shooting.

Sutton shot the gun out of the enraged man's hand, but not before one of McGrath's rounds had struck Fern in the right shoulder.

"*She* killed Dade!" McGrath screeched, clutching his bloody hand and pointing it at Fern. "You *heard* her. She *admitted* she did it."

"You want revenge against her, McGrath?" Sutton prodded.

"You're damn right I do!"

"Then testify against her in court back in Virginia City. Tell the court what you heard here. Kimball will back you up. So will I. Even Loi Yan and Kimball, I'm willing to wager, will testify. Am I right about that Loi Yan? Kimball?"

Loi Yan got to her feet, shuddered, nodded.

"I'll testify," Kimball murmured in a mournful voice, his eyes cast down.

"What about you, McGrath? You'll throw in with us?"

McGrath hesitated a moment and then in a bitter voice muttered, "I'll testify. I want to see her hang."

"I've a pretty strong feeling you will," Sutton muttered.

Fern, staring dully at the blood seeping from her flesh wound, sighed. "I could have been rich. Maybe even famous in San Francisco. Men would have flocked to my door. Jewels. Gowns. Anything I wanted—it all could have been mine." She squeezed her eyes shut and then they snapped open. "You ruined my life!" she shot at Sutton.

He turned wordlessly away from her. "We'll all head for Virginia City," he announced. "Where's your horse, McGrath?" he asked as he scooped up McGrath's gun and thrust it into his waistband.

"Back there in the woods."

"You and me, we'll go get it."

When Sutton and McGrath returned with McGrath's horse, Sutton, seeing that Kimball had bound up his wound, asked Loi Yan to do the same for Fern's injury. When Loi Yan had done so, he told her to take Proctor's horse. "I'll drape Proctor's body over its withers, if you don't mind, Loi Yan."

Later, as they rode east through the mountains with Sutton bringing up the rear, he moved up beside Kimball, who was just ahead of him, and said, "I'm glad it wasn't you I had to bring in. You treated me real decent when you found me half dead on your doorstep."

"You won't get to collect the bounty money now," Kimball commented, "since it was me they offered it for."

"You're wrong about that," Sutton said. "The bounty money's being offered to whoever can bring in the murderer of Dade McGrath. Well, I am bringing in the murderer of Dade McGrath." He pointed at Fern, who was riding ahead of them beside Loi Yan. He paused and then said, "You know something, Kimball? What you did for Miss Thorndyke—taking the blame for McGrath's killing—that was pure addlebrained foolishness. But I reckon I can understand why you did it."

"I thought Fern loved me. I thought I loved her."

"Back in San Francisco, I had me several talks with Roberta Pritchard, and I got the distinct impression that she's taken a pretty strong fancy to you. In fact, she up and admitted to me that she's fallen head over heels in love with you. Like I told you before back at your cabin, it was her who told me where you'd gone to hide out. She wanted me to take you back to stand trial in the hope that what we both thought at the time was your crime of passion would maybe get you some leniency from the court in Virginia City."

Kimball's eyes brightened. "Roberta and I—well, there was Fern, and I didn't want to be a cad, so I never let myself hope—"

"A woman like Roberta Pritchard," Sutton said, "one

that's as soft and pretty as a calf's ears—well, I got to admit how much I do envy you, Kimball."

Kimball suddenly stood up in his stirrups and let out a loud whoop of noisy joy.

"Well," Sutton mused with mock solemnity a moment later, "it sure is easy to see that Roberta's got you just about harness broke already, and the two of you aren't even hitched yet."

"Not yet, we're not," Kimball stated happily. He grinned.

So did Sutton as they rode on together.

LEO P. KELLEY has written more than a dozen novels, including the Cimarron series of Western novels, and published many short stories in leading magazines. In addition to the six Luke Sutton books, he has written a suspense novel, *Deadlocked!,* which was nominated for the Mystery Writers of America's Edgar Award.